IN EVIL HOUR

In Evil Hour

GABRIEL GARCÍA MÁRQUEZ

Translated from the Spanish by Gregory Rabassa

HarperPerennial
A Division of HarperCollinsPublishers

This work was first published in Spain under the title *La Mala Hora*. Copyright Editorial Sudamericana S.A. 1968.

Portions of this work originally appeared in *The Kenyon Review*.

A hardcover edition of this book was published in 1979 by Harper & Row, Publishers.

First HarperPerennial edition published 1991.

Designer: Sidney Feinberg

The Library of Congress has catalogued the hardcover edition as follows:
García Márquez, Gabriel, 1928–
  In evil hour.
  Translation of La mala hora.
  I. Title.
PZ4.G2164I1 [PQ8180.17.A73] 863   74-15873
ISBN 0-06-011414-2

ISBN 0-06-091964-7 (pbk.)
91 92 93 94 95 10 9 8 7 6 5 4 3 2 1

IN EVIL HOUR

FATHER ÁNGEL sat up with a solemn effort. He rubbed his eyelids with the bones of his hands, pushed aside the embroidered mosquito netting, and remained sitting on the bare mattress, pensive for an instant, the time indispensable for him to realize that he was alive and to remember the date and its corresponding day on the calendar of saints. Tuesday, October fourth, he thought; and in a low voice he said: "St. Francis of Assisi."

He got dressed without washing and without praying. He was large, ruddy, with the peaceful figure of a domesticated ox, and he moved like an ox, with thick, sad gestures. After attending to the buttoning of his cassock, with the languid attention and the movements with which a harp is tuned, he took down the bar and opened the door to the court-yard. The spikenards in the rain brought back the words of a song to him.

" 'The sea will grow larger with my tears,' " he sighed.

The bedroom was connected to the church by an inside veranda bordered with flowerpots and paved with loose bricks between which the October grass was beginning to grow. Before going into the church, Father Ángel went to the toilet. He urinated abundantly, holding his breath so as not to inhale the intense ammonia smell which brought out tears in him. Then he went out onto the veranda, remembering: "This bark will bear me to your dreams." At the narrow little door of the church he smelled the vapor of the spikenards for the last time.

Inside it smelled bad. There was a long nave, also paved with loose bricks, and with a single door opening on the square. Father Ángel went directly to the bell tower. He saw that the counterweights of the clock were more than a yard above his head and he thought that it was still wound up enough to last a week. The mosquitoes attacked him. He squashed one on the back of his neck with a violent slap and wiped his hand on the bell rope. Then from up above he heard the visceral sound of the complicated mechanical gears and immediately thereafter—dull, deep—the bell tolling five o'clock in his stomach.

He waited until the last resonance died down. Then he grabbed the rope with both hands, wrapped it around his wrists, and made the cracked bronzes ring with peremptory conviction. He had turned sixty-one years of age and the effort of ringing the bells was too strenuous for him, but he had always made the call to mass personally and that exercise strengthened his morale.

Trinidad pushed open the street door while the bells were ringing and went to the corner where she had set the traps for the mice. She found something that brought on repugnance and pleasure in her at the same time: a small massacre.

She opened the first trap, picked up the mouse by the tail

with her thumb and forefinger, and threw it into a cardboard box. Father Ángel had just opened the door onto the square.

"Good morning, Father," Trinidad said.

His baritone voice didn't register. The desolate square, the almond trees sleeping in the rain, the village motionless in the inconsolable October dawn, produced in him a feeling of abandonment. But when he grew accustomed to the sound of the rain, he made out, in the rear of the square, clear and somewhat unreal, Pastor's clarinet. Only then did he respond to the good morning.

"Pastor wasn't with the people serenading," he said.

"No," Trinidad confirmed. She approached with the box of dead mice. "It was all guitars."

"They spent almost two hours on one silly little song," the priest said. " 'The sea will grow larger with my tears.' Isn't that how it goes?"

"That's Pastor's new song," she said.

Motionless by the door, the priest experienced an instantaneous fascination. For many years he had heard Pastor's clarinet as two blocks away he would sit down to practice every day at five o'clock with his stool up against the prop of his dovecote. It was the mechanism of the town functioning with precision: first the five bell tolls of five o'clock; then the first call to mass, and then Pastor's clarinet in the courtyard of his house, purifying the pigeon-filth-laden air with diaphanous and articulated notes.

"The music is good," the priest reacted, "but the lyrics are silly. The words can roll either backward or forward and it won't make any difference: 'This bark will bear me to your dreams.' "

He turned half around, smiling at his own discovery, and went to light the altar. Trinidad followed him. She was wearing a long white robe with sleeves down to her knuckles and the blue silk sash of a lay order. Her eyes were of an intense black under the merged eyebrows.

"They were around here all night," the priest said.

"At Margot Ramírez' place," said Trinidad distractedly, shaking the dead mice in the box. "But last night there was something better than the serenade."

The priest stopped and fixed his eyes of silent blue on her.

"What was that?"

"Lampoons," said Trinidad. And she let out a nervous little laugh.

Three houses beyond, César Montero was dreaming about elephants. He'd seen them at the movies on Sunday. Rain had fallen a half hour before the film was over and now it was continuing in his dream.

César Montero turned the whole weight of his monumental body against the wall while terrified natives fled the herd of elephants. His wife pushed him softly, but neither of them woke up. "We're leaving," he murmured, and recovered his initial position. Then he woke up. At that moment the second call to mass sounded.

It was a room with large screened openings. The window on the square, also screened, had a cretonne curtain with yellow flowers. On the small night table there was a portable radio, a lamp, and a clock with a luminous dial. On the other side, against the wall, an enormous wardrobe with mirrored doors. While he was putting on his riding boots, César Montero began to hear Pastor's clarinet. The raw leather laces were stiffened with mud. He pulled hard on them, drawing them through his closed hand, which was rougher than the leather of the laces. Then he looked for his spurs, but he couldn't find them under the bed. He went on getting dressed in the dark, trying not to make any noise so as not to awaken his wife. As he was buttoning up his shirt he looked at the time on the clock on the table, then went back to looking for the spurs under the bed. First he searched for them with his hands. Progressively, he got down on all fours and started scratching under the bed. His wife woke up.

"What are you looking for?"

"The spurs."

"They're hanging behind the wardrobe," she said. "You put them there yourself on Saturday."

She pushed aside the mosquito netting and turned on the light. He stood up, shamefaced. He was monumental, with square, solid shoulders, but his movements were elastic, even when he wore his boots, the soles of which looked like two strips of wood. His health was somewhat barbarous. He seemed of an indefinite age, but the skin on his neck showed that it had gone beyond fifty. He sat on the bed to put on his spurs.

"It's still raining," she said, feeling that her aching bones had absorbed the dampness of the night. "I feel like a sponge."

Small, bony, with a long, sharp nose, she had the quality of not seeming to have finished waking up. She tried to see the rain through the curtain. César Montero finished adjusting his spurs, stood up, and stamped several times on the floor. The house shook with the copper spurs.

"The jaguar gets fat in October," he said.

But his wife, in ecstasy over Pastor's melody, didn't hear him. When she looked at him again he was combing his hair in front of the wardrobe, his legs apart and his head bent over, because he was too tall for the mirrors.

She was following Pastor's melody in a low voice.

"They were plucking that song all night long," he said.

"It's very pretty," she said.

5

She untied a ribbon from the headboard of the bed, gathered up her hair at the back of her neck, and sighed, completely awake: " 'I'll stay in your dreams until death.' " He paid no attention to her. From a drawer in the wardrobe, where, besides some jewels, there were a small woman's watch and a fountain pen, he took out a billfold with some money. He extracted four bills and returned the wallet to the same place. Then he put six shotgun shells in his shirt pocket.

"If the rain keeps up, I won't be back on Saturday," he said.

When he opened the door to the courtyard, he paused for an instant on the threshold, breathing in the somber smell of October while his eyes became accustomed to the darkness. He was going to close the door, when the alarm clock in the bedroom rang.

His wife leaped out of bed. He remained in suspense, his hand on the knob, until she turned off the alarm. Then he looked at her for the first time, pensively.

"Last night I dreamed about elephants," he said.

Then he closed the door and went to saddle up the mule.

The rain grew stronger before the third call. A low wind pulled the last rotten leaves off the almond trees on the square. The street lights went out but the houses were still locked. César Montero rode the mule into the kitchen and without dismounting, shouted to his wife to bring him his raincoat. He took off the double-barreled shotgun which he had slung over his shoulder and fastened it horizontally with the saddle straps. His wife appeared in the kitchen with the raincoat.

"Wait for it to clear," she told him without conviction.

He put the raincoat on silently. Then he looked toward the courtyard.

"It won't clear until December."

She accompanied him with her gaze to the other end of the veranda. The rain was pelting the rusty sheets on the roof, but he was going. Spurring the mule, he had to bend over in the saddle so as not to hit the crossbeam of the door as he went into the courtyard. The drops from the eaves exploded like buckshot on his back. From the main door he shouted without turning his head:

"See you Saturday."

"See you Saturday," she said.

The only door on the square that was open was that of the church. César Montero looked up and saw the sky, heavy and low, two feet above his head. He crossed himself and spurred the mule, making it whirl about several times on its hind legs until the animal got a grip on the soapy soil. That was when he saw the piece of paper stuck to the door of his house.

He read it without dismounting. The water had dissolved the colors, but the text, written with a brush in rough printed letters, could still be made out. César Montero brought the mule over to the wall, pulled off the paper, and tore it to bits.

With a slap of the reins he pressed the mule into a short trot, good for many hours. He left the square through a narrow and twisted street with adobe-walled houses whose doors turned out the dregs of sleep when they were opened. He caught the smell of coffee. Only when he left the last houses of the town behind did he turn the mule around and, with the same short and regular trot, return to the square and stop in front of Pastor's house. There he dismounted, took off the shotgun, and tied the mule to the prop, performing each action in the precise time needed.

The door was unbolted, blocked at the bottom by a giant sea shell. César Montero went into the small shadowy living room. He heard a sharp note and then an expectant silence.

He passed by four chairs arranged around a small table with a woolen cloth and a vase with artificial flowers. Finally he stopped in front of the courtyard door, threw back the hood of his raincoat, released the safety catch of the shotgun by feel, and with a calm, almost friendly voice, called:

"Pastor."

Pastor appeared in the frame of the door, screwing off the mouthpiece of the clarinet. He was a thin, straight lad with an incipient line of mustache trimmed with scissors. When he saw César Montero with his heels planted on the earthen floor and the shotgun at waist level pointed at him, Pastor opened his mouth. But he didn't say anything. He turned pale and smiled. César Montero first firmed his heels against the ground, then the butt, with his elbow, against his hip; then he clenched his teeth and, at the same time, the trigger. The house shook with the explosion, but César Montero didn't know whether it was before or after the commotion that from the other side of the door he saw Pastor dragging himself with the undulation of a worm along a furrow of tiny bloody feathers.

The mayor had begun to fall asleep at the moment of the shot. He'd spent three sleepless nights in torment because of the pain in his molar. That morning, at the first call to mass, he took his eighth analgesic. The pain gave way. The crackling of the rain on the zinc roof helped him fall asleep, but the molar was still throbbing painlessly while he slept. When he heard the shot he awoke with a leap and grabbed the cartridge belt and revolver that he always left on a chair beside the hammock, within reach of his left hand. But since he could hear only the noise of the drizzle, he thought it had been a nightmare and he felt the pain again.

He had a slight fever. In the mirror he noticed that his cheek was swelling. He opened a jar of mentholated vaseline and rubbed it on the painful part, tight and unshaven. Suddenly he caught the sound of distant voices through the rain. He went out onto the balcony. The residents of the street, some in their nightclothes, were running toward the square. A boy turned his head toward him, raised his arms, and shouted without stopping:

"César Montero has killed Pastor."

On the square, César Montero was walking around with his shotgun pointed at the crowd. The mayor recognized him with a little trouble. He took his revolver in his left hand and started forward toward the center of the square. The people made way for him. Out of the poolroom came a policeman holding his rifle, aiming at César Montero. The mayor said to him in a low voice: "Don't shoot, you animal." He holstered his revolver, took the rifle away from the policeman, and continued toward the center of the square.

"César Montero," the mayor shouted, "give me that shotgun."

César Montero hadn't seen him until then. With a leap he turned toward him. The mayor tightened his finger on the trigger, but he didn't fire.

"Come get it," César Montero shouted.

The mayor was holding the rifle with his left hand and was wiping his eyelids with the right. He calculated every step, his finger tense on the trigger and his eyes fixed on César Montero. Suddenly he stopped and spoke with a friendly cadence:

"Toss the shotgun on the ground, César. Don't do anything else foolish."

César Montero drew back. The mayor continued on, his finger tight on the trigger. He didn't move a single muscle in his body until César Montero lowered the shotgun and dropped it. Then the mayor realized that he was wearing only his pajama bottoms, that he was sweating in the rain, and that his tooth had stopped aching.

The houses opened up. Two policemen armed with rifles ran to the center of the square. The crowd poured in behind them. The policemen leaped in a half turn and shouted, pointing their rifles:

"Back."

The mayor shouted in a calm voice, not looking at anyone:

"Clear the square."

The crowd dispersed. The mayor frisked César Montero without making him take off his raincoat. He found four shells in his shirt pocket, and in the back pants pocket a switchblade knife with a bone handle. In another pocket he found a notebook, a ring with three keys, and four one-hundred-peso bills. Impassively, César Montero let himself be searched, his arms open, moving his body only to facilitate the operation. When he was finished, the mayor called the two policemen, gave them the things, and turned César Montero over to them.

"Take him to the second floor of the town hall," he ordered. "I'm holding you responsible for him."

César Montero took off the raincoat. He gave it to one of the policemen and walked between them, indifferent to the rain and the perplexity of the people concentrated on the square. The mayor, thoughtfully, watched him go away. Then he turned to the crowd, made a gesture of shooing chickens, and shouted:

"Break it up."

Drying his face with his bare arm, he crossed the square and went into Pastor's house.

Collapsed in a chair was the dead man's mother, in the midst of women fanning her with pitiless diligence. The mayor pushed a woman aside. "Give her air," he said. The woman turned toward him.

"She'd just left for mass," she said.

"All right," the mayor said, "but now let her breathe."

Pastor was on the porch, face down by the dovecote, on a bed of bloody feathers. There was an intense smell of pigeon filth. A group of men were trying to lift the body when the mayor appeared in the doorway.

"Back off," he said.

The men put the body back down among the feathers, in the same position that they had found it, and withdrew silently. After examining the body, the mayor rolled it over. There was a dispersion of tiny feathers. At waist level there were more feathers, sticking to the still warm and living blood. He pushed them away with his hands. The shirt was torn and the belt buckle broken. Underneath the shirt he saw the disclosed viscera. The wound had stopped bleeding.

"It was with a jaguar gun," one of the men said.

The mayor stood up. He cleaned off the bloody feathers on a prop of the dovecote, still looking at the corpse. He ended by wiping his hand on his pajama pants and said to the group:

"Don't move him from there."

"He's going to leave him stretched out there," one of the men said.

"We have to draw up the removal document," the mayor said.

Inside the house the wailing of the women began. The mayor made his way through the shouts and the suffocating smells that were beginning to cut off the air in the room. At the street door he ran into Father Ángel.

"He's dead," the priest exclaimed, perplexed.

"Dead as a pig," the mayor answered.

The houses around the square were open. The rain had stopped but the heavy sky floated over the roofs without so much as a chink for the sun. Father Ángel held the mayor back by the arm.

"César Montero is a good man," he said. "This must have been a moment of confusion."

"I know that," the mayor said impatiently. "Don't worry, Father, nothing's going to happen to him. Go inside; that's where they need you."

He went away with a certain haste and ordered the policemen to call off the guard. The crowd, held back behind a line until then, ran toward Pastor's house. The mayor went into the poolroom, where a policeman was waiting for him with a set of clean clothing: his lieutenant's uniform.

Ordinarily the establishment wasn't open at that hour. On that day, before seven o'clock, it was crowded. Around the tables which seated four or against the bar, men were drinking coffee. Most of them still wore their pajama tops and slippers.

The mayor got undressed in front of everyone, half dried himself with the pajama pants, and began to dress in silence, hanging on the comments. When he left the place he was completely informed of the details of the incident.

"Have a care," he shouted from the door. "Anybody who stirs up the town on me I'll clap in the poky."

He went down the stone-paved street without saying hello to anyone but aware of the town's excited state. He was young, with relaxed movements, and with every step he revealed his aim of making his presence felt.

At seven o'clock the launches that carried cargo and passengers three times a week whistled as they left the pier, with no one paying the attention they did on other days. The mayor went down along the arcade, where the Syrian merchants were beginning to display their colorful wares. Dr. Octavio Giraldo, an ageless physician with a headful of patent leather curls, was watching the launches go downstream from the door of his office. He, too, was wearing his pajama top and slippers.

"Doctor," the mayor said, "get dressed so you can go perform the autopsy."

The doctor looked at him, intrigued. He revealed a long row of solid white teeth. "So we're doing autopsies now," he said, and added:

"That's great progress, obviously."

The mayor tried to smile, but the sensitivity of his cheek prevented it. He covered his mouth with his hand.

"What's the matter?" the doctor asked.

"A bastardly molar."

Dr. Giraldo seemed disposed to conversation. But the mayor was in a hurry.

At the end of the dock he knocked on the door of a house that had walls of ditch reeds without mud and a palm roof that came down almost to water level. A woman with greenish skin, seven months pregnant, opened for him. She was barefoot. The mayor pushed her to one side and went into the shadowy living room.

"Judge," he called.

Judge Arcadio appeared at the inside door, dragging his clogs. He was wearing drill pants, with no belt, held up under his navel and naked torso.

"Get a body removal form ready," the mayor said.

Judge Arcadio gave a whistle of perplexity.

"Where did you get that novel idea from?"

The mayor followed him slowly into the bedroom. "This is different," he said, opening the window to purify the sleep-laden air. "It's best to do things properly." He wiped the dust from his hands onto his pressed pants and asked, without the slightest indication of sarcasm:

"Do you know what a body removal order is?"

"Of course," the judge said.

The mayor examined his hands at the window. "Get your secretary so he can do what writing there is," he said, again with no veiled intention. Then he turned toward the girl, the palms of his hands held out. There were traces of blood.

"Where can I wash?"

"In the tank," she said.

The mayor went out into the courtyard. The girl looked in the chest for a clean towel and wrapped a cake of scented soap in it.

She went out into the courtyard just as the mayor was returning to the bedroom shaking his hands.

"I was bringing you the soap," she said.

"It's all right this way," the mayor said. He looked at the palms of his hands again. He took the towel and dried himself, pensive, looking at Judge Arcadio.

"He was covered with pigeon feathers," he said.

Sitting on the bed, taking measured sips from a cup of black coffee, he waited until Judge Arcadio finished getting dressed. The girl followed them through the living room.

"Until that molar's pulled out, the swelling won't go down," she said to the mayor.

He pushed Judge Arcadio out into the street, turned to look at her, and touched her bulging belly with his forefinger.

"What about this swelling? When will it go down?"

"Any day now," she said.

Father Ángel didn't take his customary evening walk. After the funeral he stopped to chat at a house in the lower part of town and stayed there until dusk. He felt well, in spite of the fact that the prolonged rains ordinarily brought on pain in his spine. When he got home the street lights were on.

Trinidad was watering the flowers on the porch. The priest asked her about the unconsecrated hosts and she answered that she'd put them on the main altar. The fog of mosquitoes enveloped him when he lighted the lamp in his room. Before closing the door he fumigated the room endlessly with insecticide, sneezing because of the smell. He was sweating when he finished. He changed the black cassock for the white mended one that he wore in private and went to ring the Angelus.

Back in the room, he put a pan on the fire and started frying a piece of meat while he sliced an onion. Then he put everything on a plate where there was a piece of marinated cassava and some cold rice, leftovers from lunch. He took the plate to the table and sat down to eat.

He ate it all at the same time, cutting little pieces of everything and piling them on his fork with the knife. He chewed conscientiously, grinding everything down to the last grain with his silver-capped molars, but with his lips closed. While he did so, he left the knife and fork on the edges of the plate and examined the room with a continuous and perfectly attentive look. Opposite him were the shelves with the thick books of the parish archives. In the corner a wicker rocking chair with a tall back and a cushion sewn on at head level. Behind the rocker there was a screen with a crucifix hanging on it next to a calendar advertising cough medicine. On the other side of the screen was his bedroom.

At the end of his meal, Father Ángel felt asphyxiated. He unwrapped a morsel of guava paste, filled his glass up to the brim with water, and ate the sugary sweet looking at the calendar. Between each mouthful he took a sip of water, without taking his eyes off the calendar. Finally he belched and wiped his lips with his sleeve. For nineteen years he had eaten that way, alone in his study, repeating every movement with scrupulous precision. He'd never felt ashamed of his solitude.

After rosary, Trinidad asked him for money to buy arsenic. The priest refused for the third time, arguing that the traps were sufficient. Trinidad insisted:

"It's just that the littlest mice steal the cheese and don't get caught in the traps. That's why it's best to poison the cheese."

The priest admitted to himself that Trinidad was right. But before he could express it, the noisy loudspeaker at the movie theater across the street penetrated the quiet of the church. First it was a dull growl. Then the scratching of the needle on the record and immediately a mambo that started off with a strident trumpet.

"Is there a show tonight?" the priest asked.

Trinidad said there was.

"Do you know what they're showing?"

"Tarzan and the Green Goddess," Trinidad said. "The same one they couldn't finish on Sunday because of the rain. Approved for all."

Father Ángel went to the bottom of the belfry and tolled the bell twelve slow times. Trinidad was puzzled.

"You're wrong, Father," she said, waving her hands and with an agitated glow in her eyes. "It's a movie that's approved for all. Remember, you didn't ring the bell once on Sunday."

"But it's a lack of consideration for the town," the priest said, drying the sweat on his neck. And he repeated, panting: "A lack of consideration."

Trinidad understood.

"All you had to do was to have seen that funeral," the priest said. "All the men fighting for a chance to carry the coffin."

Then he sent the girl off, closed the door to the deserted

square, and put out the lights in the church. On the porch, on his way back to his bedroom, he slapped his forehead, remembering that he'd forgotten to give Trinidad the money for the arsenic. But he'd forgotten about it again before he reached his room.

A short time later, sitting at his desk, he got ready to finish the letter he'd begun the night before. He'd unbuttoned his cassock down to his stomach and was putting the writing pad, the inkwell, and the blotter in order on the desk while he reached in his pockets for his glasses. Then he remembered having left them in the cassock that he'd worn to the funeral and got up to get them. He'd reread what he'd written the night before and started a new paragraph when three knocks sounded on the door.

"Come in."

It was the manager of the movie house. Small, pale, very clean-shaven, he wore an expression of fatality. He was dressed in white linen, spotless, and was wearing two-toned shoes. Father Ángel signaled him to sit in the wicker rocking chair, but he took a handkerchief out of his pants, unfolded it scrupulously, dusted off the step, and sat down with his legs apart. Father Ángel saw then that it wasn't a revolver but a flashlight that he wore in his belt.

"What can I do for you?" the priest asked.

"Father," the manager said, almost breathless, "forgive me for butting into your affairs, but tonight it must have been a mistake."

The priest nodded his head and waited.

"*Tarzan and the Green Goddess* is a movie approved for all," the manager went on. "You yourself recognized that on Sunday."

The priest tried to interrupt him, but the manager raised one hand as a signal that he hadn't finished yet.

"I've accepted the business of the bell," he said, "because it's true, there are immoral movies. But there's nothing wrong with this one. We intended to show it on Saturday for the children's matinee."

Father Ángel explained to him then that, indeed, the movie had no moral classification on the list that he received in the mail every month.

"But having a movie today," he went on, "shows a lack of consideration since there's been a death in town. That, too, is a part of morality."

The manager looked at him.

"Last year the police themselves killed a man inside the movies and as soon as they took the body out the show went on," he exclaimed.

"It's different now," the priest said. "The mayor's a changed man."

"When they hold elections again the killing will come back," the manager replied, exasperated. "Always, ever since the town has been a town, the same thing happens."

"We'll see," the priest said.

The manager examined him with a look of grief. When he spoke again, shaking his shirt to ventilate his chest, his voice had acquired a tone of supplication.

"It's the third movie approved for all that we've had this year," he said. "On Sunday three reels were left because of the rain and there are a lot of people who want to know how it comes out."

"The bell has already been rung," the priest said.

The manager let out a sigh of desperation. He waited, looking at the prelate face on and no longer thinking about anything except the intense heat in the study.

"So there's nothing that can be done?"

Father Ángel shook his head.

The manager slapped his knees and got up.

"All right," he said. "What can we do."

He folded his handkerchief again, dried the sweat on his neck, and examined the study with bitter care.

"This place is an inferno," he said.

The priest accompanied him to the door. He threw the bolt and sat down to finish the letter. After reading it again from the beginning, he completed the interrupted paragraph and stopped to think. At that moment the music from the loudspeaker stopped. "We would like to announce to our distinguished clientele," an impersonal voice said, "that tonight's show has been canceled because this establishment also wishes to join the town in mourning." Father Ángel, smiling, recognized the manager's voice.

The heat grew more intense. The curate continued writing, with brief pauses to dry his sweat and reread what he had written, until two sheets were filled. He had just signed it when the rain let loose without warning. A vapor of damp earth penetrated the room. Father Ángel addressed the envelope, closed the inkwell, and was ready to fold the letter. But first he read the last paragraph over again. Then he opened the inkwell and wrote a postscript: *It's raining again. With this winter and the things I've told you about, I think that bitter days await us.*

ℱRIDAY DAWNED warm and dry. Judge Arcadio, who boasted of having made love three times a night ever since he'd made it for the first time, broke the cords of the mosquito netting that morning and fell to the floor with his wife at the supreme moment, wrapped up in the embroidered canopy.

"Leave it the way it is," she murmured. "I'll fix it later."

They arose completely naked from the midst of the confused nebula of the mosquito net. Judge Arcadio went to the chest to get some clean underwear. When he got back his wife was dressed, putting the mosquito netting in order. He passed by without looking at her and sat down on the other side of the bed to put his shoes on, his breathing still heavy from love. She pursued him. She rested her round, tense stomach against his arm and sought his ear with her teeth. He pushed her away softly.

"Leave me alone," he said.

She let out a laugh loaded with good health. She followed her husband to the other side of the room, poking her forefingers into his kidneys. "Giddy-ap, donkey," she said. He gave a leap and pushed her hands away. She left him alone and laughed again, but suddenly she became serious and shouted:

"Oh, my God!"

"What is it?" he asked.

"The door was wide open," she shouted. "That's the limit of shamelessness."

She went into the bathroom bursting with laughter.

Judge Arcadio didn't wait for breakfast. Comforted by the mint in his toothpaste, he went out onto the street. There was a copper sun. The Syrians sitting by the doors of their shops were contemplating the peaceful river. As he passed by Dr. Giraldo's office he scratched his nail on the screen of the door and shouted without stopping:

"Doctor, what's the best cure for a headache?"

The physician answered from inside:

"Not having drunk anything the night before."

At the dock a group of women were commenting in loud voices about the contents of a new lampoon nailed up the night before. Since the day had dawned clear and rainless, the women who went by on their way to five o'clock mass had read it and now the whole town was informed. Judge Arcadio didn't stop. He felt like an ox with a ring in his nose being led to the poolroom. There he asked for a cold beer and an aspirin. It had just struck nine but the establishment was already full.

"The whole town has a headache," Judge Arcadio said.

He took the bottle to a table where three men seemed perplexed over their glasses of beer. He sat down in the empty seat.

"Is that mess still going on?" he asked.

"There were four of them this morning."

"The one everybody read," one of the men said, "was the one about Raquel Contreras."

Judge Arcadio swallowed the aspirin and drank his beer from the bottle. The first swallow was distasteful, but then his stomach adjusted and he felt new and without a past.

"What did it say?"

"Foolishness," the man said. "That the trips she took this year weren't to get her dentures fitted, as she said, but to get an abortion."

"They didn't have to go to the trouble of putting up a lampoon," Judge Arcadio said. "Everybody was going around saying that."

Even though the hot sun hurt him in the depths of his eyes when he left the establishment, he didn't feel the confused queasiness of dawn then. He went directly to the courthouse. His secretary, a skinny old man who was plucking a chicken, received him over the frames of his glasses with a look of incredulity.

"To what do we owe this miracle?"

"We have to get this mess in order," the judge said.

The secretary went out into the courtyard, dragging his slippers, and he handed the half-plucked chicken over the wall to the cook at the hotel. Eleven months after taking over his post, Judge Arcadio had settled himself at his desk for the first time.

The run-down office was divided into two sections by a wooden railing. In the outer section there was a platform, also of wood, under the picture of Justice blindfolded with a scale in her hand. Inside, two old desks facing each other, some shelves with dusty books, and the typewriter. On the wall over the judge's desk, a copper crucifix. On the wall opposite, a framed lithograph: a smiling, fat, bald man, his chest crossed by the presidential sash, and underneath a gilt inscription: *Peace and Justice*. The lithograph was the only new thing in the office.

The secretary wrapped a handkerchief around his face and began to clean the desks with a duster. "If you don't cover your nose, you'll get a coughing attack," he said. The advice wasn't taken. Judge Arcadio leaned back in the swivel chair, stretching out his legs to test the springs.

"Will it fall over?" he asked.

The secretary said no with his head. "When they killed Judge Vitela," he said, "the springs broke, but they've been fixed." Without taking off the kerchief, he went on:

"The mayor himself ordered it fixed when the government changed and special investigators began to appear from all sides."

"The mayor wants this office to function," the judge said.

He opened the center drawer, took out a bunch of keys, and went on opening the drawers one by one. They were full of papers. He examined them superficially, picking them up with his forefinger to be sure that there was nothing to attract his attention, and then he closed the drawers and put the items on the desk in order: a glass inkwell with one red and one blue receptacle, and a fountain pen for each receptacle, of the respective color. The ink had dried up.

"The mayor likes you," the secretary said.

Rocking in his chair, the judge followed him with a somber look as he cleaned the railing. The secretary contemplated him as if he never meant to forget him under that light, at that instant, and in that position, and he said, pointing at him with his finger:

"Just the way you are now, exactly, was how Judge Vitela was when they shot him up."

The judge touched the pronounced veins on his temples. The headache was coming back.

"I was there," the secretary went on, pointing to the typewriter, as he went to the other side of the railing. Without interrupting his tale, he leaned on the railing with the duster aimed at Judge Arcadio like a rifle. He looked like a mail robber in a cowboy movie.

"The three policemen stood like this," he said. "Judge Vitela just managed to see them and raise his hands, saying very slowly: 'Don't kill me.' But right away the chair went in one direction and he in the other, riddled with lead."

Judge Arcadio squeezed his skull with his hands. He felt his brain throbbing. The secretary took off his mask and hung the duster behind the door. "And all because when he was drunk he said he was here to guarantee the sanctity of the ballot," he said. He remained suspended, looking at Judge Arcadio, who doubled over the desk with his hands on his stomach.

"Are you having trouble?"

The judge said he was. He told him about the night before and asked him to go to the poolroom and get an aspirin and two cold beers. When he finished the first beer, Judge Arcadio couldn't find the slightest trace of remorse in his heart. He was lucid.

The secretary sat in front of the typewriter.

"What do we do now?" he asked.

"Nothing," the judge said.

"Then if you'll allow me, I'll go find María and help her pluck the chickens."

The judge was against it. "This is an office for the administration of justice and not the plucking of chickens," he said. He examined his underling from top to bottom with an air of pity and added:

"Furthermore, you've got to get rid of those slippers and come to the office with shoes on."

The heat became more intense with the approach of

noon. When twelve o'clock struck, Judge Arcadio had consumed a dozen beers. He was floating in memories. With a dreamy anxiety he was talking about a past without privations, with long Sundays of sea and insatiable mulatto women who made love standing up behind the doors of entranceways. "That's what life was like then," he said, snapping his thumb against his forefinger at the clamlike stupor of the secretary, who listened without speaking, approving with his head. Judge Arcadio felt dull, but ever more alive in his memories.

When one o'clock sounded in the belfry, the secretary showed signs of impatience.

"The soup's getting cold," he said.

The judge wouldn't let him get up. "A person doesn't always come across a man of talent in towns like this," he said, and the secretary thanked him, worn out by the heat, and shifted in his chair. It was an interminable Friday. Under the burning plates of the roof, the two men chatted a half hour more while the town cooked in its siesta stew. On the edge of exhaustion, the secretary then made a reference to the lampoons. Judge Arcadio shrugged his shoulders.

"So you're following that half-wit stuff too," he said, using the familiar form for the first time.

The secretary had no desire to go on chatting, debilitated by hunger and suffocation, but he didn't think the lampoons were foolishness. "We've already had the first death," he said. "If things go on like this we're going to have a bad time of it." And he told the story of a town that was wiped out in seven days by lampoons. The inhabitants ended up killing each other off. The survivors dug up the bones of their dead and carried them off to be sure they'd never come back.

The judge listened with an amused expression, slowly unbuttoning his shirt while the other talked. He figured that his secretary was a horror-story fan.

"This is a very simple case out of a detective story," he said.

The underling shook his head. Judge Arcadio told how he'd belonged to an organization at the university that was dedicated to the solving of police enigmas. Each one of the members would read a mystery novel up to a predetermined clue, and they would get together on Saturdays to unravel the enigma. "I didn't miss a single time," he said. "Of course, I was favored by my knowledge of the classics, which had revealed a logic of life capable of penetrating any mystery." He offered an enigma: a man registers at a hotel at ten at night, goes up to his room, and the next morning the waiter who brings him his coffee finds him dead and rotting in his bed. The autopsy shows that the guest who arrived the night before has been dead for a week.

The secretary sat up with a long creaking of joints.

"That means that when he got to the hotel he had already been dead for seven days," the secretary said.

"The story was written twelve years ago," Judge Arcadio said, ignoring the interruption, "but the clue had been given by Heraclitus, five centuries before Christ."

He got ready to reveal it, but the secretary was exasperated. "Never, since the world has been the world, has anyone found out who's putting up the lampoons," he proclaimed with tense aggressiveness. Judge Arcadio contemplated him with twisted eyes.

"I bet you I'll discover him," he said.

"I accept your bet."

Rebeca Asís was suffocating in the hot bedroom of the house opposite, her head sunk in the pillow, trying to sleep an impossible siesta. She had smoked leaves stuck to her temples.

"Roberto," she said, addressing her husband, "if you

don't open the window we're going to die of the heat."

Roberto Asís opened the window at the moment in which Judge Arcadio was leaving his office.

"Try to sleep," he begged the exuberant woman who was lying with her arms open beneath the canopy of pink embroidery, completely naked under a light nylon nightgown. "I promise you I won't remember anything again."

She let out a sigh.

Roberto Asís, who had spent the night walking about the bedroom, lighting one cigarette with the butt of another, unable to sleep, had been on the point of catching the author of the lampoons that dawn. He'd heard the crackle of the paper in front of his house and the repeated rubbing of hands trying to smooth it on the wall. But he grasped it all too late and the lampoon had been posted. When he opened the window the square was deserted.

From that moment until two in the afternoon, when he promised his wife he wouldn't remember the lampoon again, she'd used every form of persuasion to try to calm him down. Finally she proposed a desperate formula: as the final proof of her innocence, she offered to confess to Father Ángel aloud and in the presence of her husband. The very offering of that humiliation had been sufficient. In spite of his confusion, he didn't dare take the next step and he had to give in.

"It's always better to talk things out," she said without opening her eyes. "It would have been a disaster if you'd stayed with your belly all tight."

He fastened the door as he went out. In the spacious shadowed house, completely shut up, he perceived the hum of his mother's electric fan, as she slept her siesta in the house next door. He poured himself a glass of lemonade from the refrigerator, under the drowsy look of the black cook.

From her cool personal surroundings the woman asked him if he wanted some lunch. He took the cover off the pot. A whole turtle was floating flippers up in the boiling water. For once he didn't shudder at the idea that the animal had been thrown alive into the pot, and that its heart would still be beating when they brought it quartered to the table.

"I'm not hungry," he said, covering the pot. And he added from the door: "The mistress won't have lunch either. She's had a headache all day."

The two houses were connected by a porch with green paving stones from where one could see the wires of the henhouse at the back of the common courtyard. In the part of the porch that belonged to his mother's house there were several birdcages hanging from the eaves and several pots with intensely colored flowers.

From the chaise longue where she had just taken her siesta, his eleven-year-old daughter greeted him with a grumbling greeting. She still had the weave of the linen marked on her cheek.

"It's going on three," he pointed out in a very low voice. And he added melancholically: "Try to keep track of things."

"I dreamed about a glass cat," the child said.

He couldn't repress a slight shudder.

"What was it like?"

"All glass," the girl said, trying to give form to the dream animal with her hands, "like a glass bird, but a cat."

He found himself lost, in full sunlight, in a strange city. "Forget about it," he murmured. "Something like that isn't worth the trouble." At that moment he saw his mother in the door of her bedroom and he felt rescued.

"You're feeling better," he asserted.

The widow Asís returned a bitter expression. "Every day

I'm getting better and better so I can vote," she com-
plained, making a bun of her abundant iron-colored hair.
She went out onto the porch to change the water in the
cages.

Roberto Asís dropped onto the chaise longue where his
daughter had been sleeping. The back of his neck in his
hands, he followed with his withered eyes the bony woman
in black who was conversing with the birds in a low voice.
They fluttered in the fresh water, sprinkling the woman's
face with their happy flapping. When she had finished with
the cages, the widow Asís wrapped her son in an aura of
uncertainty.

"You had things to do in the woods," she said.

"I didn't go," he said. "I had some things to do here."

"You won't go now till Monday."

With his eyes, he agreed. A black servant, barefoot,
crossed the room with the child to take her to school. The
widow Asís remained on the porch until they left. Then she
motioned to her son and he followed her into the broad
bedroom where the fan was humming. She dropped into a
broken-down reed rocker beside the fan with an air of extreme weariness. On the whitewashed walls hung photographs of ancient children framed in copper. Roberto Asís
stretched out on the sumptuous, regal bed where, decrepit
and in a bad humor, some of the children in the photographs, including his own father last December, had died.

"What's going on with you?" the widow asked.

"Do you believe what people are saying?" he asked in
turn.

"At my age you have to believe everything," the widow
replied. And she asked indolently: "What are they saying?"

"That Rebeca Isabel isn't my child."

The widow began to rock slowly. "She's got the Asís

nose," she said. After thinking a moment, she asked distractedly: "Who says so?" Roberto Asís bit his nails.

"They put up a lampoon."

Only then did the widow understand that the dark shadows under her son's eyes weren't the sediment of long sleeplessness.

"Lampoons are not the people," she proclaimed.

"But they only tell what people are already saying," said Roberto Asís, "even if a person doesn't know."

She, however, knew everything that the town had said about her family for many years. In a house like hers, full of servants, godchildren, and wards of all ages, it was impossible to lock oneself up in a bedroom without the rumors of the streets reaching even there. The turbulent Asíses, founders of the town when they were nothing but swineherds, seemed to have blood that was sweet for gossip.

"Everything they say isn't true," she said, "even though a person might know."

"Everybody knows that Rosario Montero was going to bed with Pastor," he said. "His last song was dedicated to her."

"Everybody said so, but nobody knew for sure," the widow replied. "On the other hand, now it's known that the song was for Margot Ramírez. They were going to be married and only they and Pastor's mother knew it. It would have been better if they hadn't guarded so jealously the only secret that's ever been kept in this town."

Roberto Asís looked at his mother with a dramatic liveliness. "There was a moment this morning when I thought I was going to die," he said. The widow didn't seem moved.

"The Asíses are jealous," she said. "That's been the great misfortune of this house."

They remained silent for a long time. It was almost four

o'clock and the heat was beginning to subside. When Roberto Asís turned off the fan the whole house was awakening, full of female voices and bird flutes.

"Pass me the bottle that's on the night table," the widow said.

She took two pills, gray and round like two artificial pearls, and gave the bottle back to her son, saying: "Take two; they'll help you sleep." He took them with the water his mother had left in the glass and rested his head on the pillow.

The widow sighed. She maintained a pensive silence. Then, as always, generalizing about the whole town when thinking of the half-dozen families that made up her class, she said:

"The worst part about this town is that the women have to stay home alone while the men go off into the woods."

Roberto Asís began to fall asleep. The widow observed his unshaven chin, the long nose made of angular cartilage, and thought about her dead husband. Adalberto Asís, too, had known despair. He was a giant woodsman who had worn a celluloid collar for fifteen minutes in his lifetime so they could take the daguerreotype that survived him on the night table. It was said of him that in that same bedroom he'd murdered a man he found sleeping with his wife, that he'd buried him secretly in the courtyard. The truth was different: Adalberto Asís had, with a shotgun blast, killed a monkey he'd caught masturbating on the bedroom beam with his eyes fixed on his wife while she was changing her clothes. He'd died forty years later without having been able to rectify the legend.

Father Ángel went up the steep stairs with open steps. On the second floor, at the end of a corridor with rifles and cartridge belts hanging on the wall, a policeman was lying on an army cot, reading face up. He was so absorbed in his reading that he didn't notice the presence of the priest until he greeted him. He rolled the magazine and sat up on the cot.

"What are you reading?" Father Ángel asked.

The policeman showed him the magazine.

"Terry and the Pirates."

With a steady look the priest examined the three cells of reinforced concrete, without windows, closed up on the corridor with thick iron bars. In the center cell another policeman was sleeping in his shorts, spread out in a hammock. The others were empty. Father Ángel asked about César Montero.

"He's in there," the policeman said, nodding his head toward a closed door. "It's the commandant's room."

"Can I talk to him?"

"He's incommunicado," the policeman said.

Father Ángel didn't insist. He asked if the prisoner was all right. The policeman answered that he'd been given the best room in the barracks, with good light and running water, but he'd gone twenty-four hours without eating. He'd refused the food the mayor had ordered from the hotel.

"They should have brought him food from home," the priest said.

"He doesn't want them to bother his wife."

As if speaking to himself, the priest murmured: "I'll talk about all this with the mayor." He started to go on toward the end of the corridor, where the mayor had built his armored office.

"He's not there," the policeman said. "He's been home two days with a toothache."

Father Ángel visited him. He was prostrate in a hammock, next to a chair where there was a jar of salt water, a package of painkillers, and the cartridge belt with the revolver. His cheek was still swollen. Father Ángel brought a chair over to the hammock.

"Have it pulled," he said.

The mayor spat a mouthful of salt water into a basin. "That's easy to say," he said, his head still leaning over the basin. Father Ángel understood. He said in a very low voice:

"If you'll authorize me, I'll talk to the dentist." He took a deep breath and ventured to add: "He's an understanding man."

"Like a mule," the mayor said. "You'd have to break him down with bullets and then we'd be back where we started."

Father Ángel followed him with his eyes to the washstand. The mayor turned on the faucet, put his swollen cheek under the flow of cool water, and held it there for an instant, with an expression of ecstasy. Then he chewed an analgesic tablet and took some water from the spigot, throwing it into his mouth with his hands.

"Seriously," the priest insisted, "I can talk to the dentist."

The mayor made a gesture of impatience.

"Do whatever you want, Father."

He lay face up in the hammock, his eyes closed, his hands behind his neck, breathing with a wrathful rhythm. The pain began to give way. When he opened his eyes again, Father Ángel was looking at him silently, sitting beside the hammock.

"What brought you over here?" the mayor asked.

"César Montero," the priest said without any preamble. "The man has to confess."

"He's incommunicado," the mayor said. "Tomorrow, after the preliminary hearing, you can confess him. He's got to be sent off on Monday."

"He's got forty-eight hours," the priest said.

"And I've had this tooth for two weeks," said the mayor.

In the dark room the mosquitoes were beginning to buzz. Father Ángel looked out the window and saw an intense pink cloud floating on the river.

"What about the meal problem?" he asked.

The mayor left his hammock to close the balcony door. "I did my duty," he said. "He doesn't want to bother his wife or have food sent from the hotel." He began to spray insecticide around the room. Father Ángel looked in his pocket for a handkerchief so as not to sneeze, but instead of the handkerchief he found a wrinkled letter. "Agh," he exclaimed, trying to smooth out the letter with his fingers. The mayor interrupted his fumigation. The priest covered his nose, but it was a useless effort: he sneezed twice. "Sneeze, Father," the mayor said. And he emphasized with a smile:

"We're living in a democracy."

Father Ángel also smiled. Showing the sealed envelope, he said: "I forgot to mail this letter." He found the hand-kerchief up his sleeve and blew his nose, irritated by the insecticide. He was still thinking about César Montero.

"It's as if you had him on bread and water," he said.

"If that's what he wants," the mayor said, "we can't force him to eat."

"What bothers me most is his conscience," the priest said.

Without taking his handkerchief away from his nose, he followed the mayor around the room with his eyes until he finished fumigating. "He must be very upset if he thinks he's going to be poisoned," he said. The mayor put the spray can on the floor.

"He knows that everybody loved Pastor," he said.

"César Montero too," the priest replied.

"But it so happens that it's Pastor who's dead."

The priest contemplated the letter. The light was becoming hazy. "Pastor," he murmured. "He didn't have time to confess." The mayor turned on the light before getting into the hammock.

"I'll feel better tomorrow," he said. "You can confess him after the proceedings. Does that suit you?"

Father Ángel agreed. "It's just for the repose of his conscience," he repeated. He stood up with a solemn movement. He recommended to the mayor that he not take too many painkillers, and the mayor answered back reminding him not to forget the letter.

"And something else, Father," the mayor said. "Try in any way you can to talk to the tooth-puller." He looked at the curate, who was beginning to go down the stairs, and added as before, smiling: "This all contributes to the consolidation of peace."

Sitting by the door of his office, the postmaster watched the afternoon die. When Father Ángel gave him the letter, he went into his office, moistened with his tongue a fifteen-centavo stamp, for airmail and the surcharge for construction. He kept on digging in his desk drawer. When the street lights went on, the priest put several coins on the counter and left without saying goodbye.

The postmaster was still searching in the drawer. A moment later, tired of rummaging through papers, he wrote on the corner of the envelope in ink: *No five-centavo stamps on hand.* He signed underneath and put the stamp of the office there.

That night, after rosary, Father Ángel found a dead mouse floating in the holy water font. Trinidad was setting the traps in the baptistery. The priest grabbed the animal by the tip of the tail.

"You're going to cause trouble," he told Trinidad, waving the dead mouse in front of her. "Don't you know that some of the faithful bottle holy water to give their sick to drink?"

"What's that got to do with it?" Trinidad asked.

"Got to do with it?" the priest answered. "Well, just that the sick people will be drinking holy water with arsenic in it."

Trinidad reminded him that he still hadn't given her the money for the arsenic. "It's plaster," she said, and revealed the method: she had put plaster in the corners of the church, the mouse ate some and a moment later, desperately thirsty, it had gone to drink at the font. The water solidified the plaster in its stomach.

"In any case," the priest said, "it would be better if you came and got the money for arsenic. I don't want any more dead mice in the holy water."

In the study a delegation of Catholic Dames was waiting for him, headed by Rebeca Asís. After giving Trinidad the money for the arsenic, the priest commented on the heat in the room and sat down at the desk facing the three Dames, who were waiting in silence.

"At your service, my distinguished ladies."

They looked at each other. Rebeca Asís then opened a fan with a Japanese landscape painted on it, and said without mystery:

"It's the matter of the lampoons, Father."

With a sinuous voice, as if she were telling a fairy tale, she recounted the alarm of the people. She said that even though Pastor's death could be interpreted "as something entirely personal," respectable families felt obliged to be concerned about the lampoons.

Leaning on her parasol, Adalgisa Montoya, the oldest of the three, was more explicit:

"We Catholic Dames have decided to intervene in the matter."

Father Ángel reflected for a few seconds. Rebeca Asís took a deep breath, and the priest wondered how that woman could exhale such a hot smell. She was splendid and floral, possessing a dazzling whiteness and passionate health. The priest spoke, his gaze fixed on an indefinite point.

"My feeling," he said, "is that we shouldn't pay any attention to the voice of scandal. We should place ourselves above such things and go on observing God's law as we have done up to now."

Adalgisa Montoya approved with a movement of her head. But the others didn't agree: it seemed to them that "this calamity can bring fatal consequences in the long run." At that moment the loudspeaker at the movie theater coughed. Father Ángel slapped his forehead. "Excuse me," he said, while he searched in the drawer for the Catholic censorship list.

"What are they showing?"

"Pirates of Space," said Rebeca Asís. "It's a war picture."

Father Ángel looked for it in the alphabetical listing, muttering fragmentary titles while he ran his index finger over the long classified list. He stopped to turn the page.

"Pirates of Space."

He was running his finger horizontally, looking for the moral classification, when he heard the voice of the manager instead of the expected record, announcing the cancellation of the performance because of bad weather. One of the women explained that the manager had made that decision in view of the fact that the public demanded its money back if rain interrupted the movie before it was half over.

"Too bad," Father Ángel said. "It was approved for all."

He closed the notebook and continued:

"As I was saying, this is an observant town. Nineteen years ago, when they assigned me to the parish, there were eleven cases of public concubinage among the important families. Today there is only one left and I hope for a short time only."

"It's not for us," Rebeca Asís said. "But these poor people . . ."

"There's no cause for worry," the priest went on, indifferent to the interruption. "One has to remember how much the town has changed. In those days a Russian ballerina gave a show for men only in the cockpit and at the end she auctioned off everything she was wearing."

Adalgisa Montoya interrupted him.

"That's just the way it was," she said.

Indeed, she remembered the scandal as it had been told to her: when the dancer was completely naked, an old man began to shout from the stands, went up to the top bench, and urinated all over the audience. They'd told her that the rest of the men, following his example, had ended up urinating on each other in the midst of maddening shouts.

"Now," the priest went on, "it's been proven that this is the most observant town in the whole apostolic prefecture."

He elaborated his thesis. He referred to some difficult instances in his struggle against the debilities and weaknesses of the human species, until the Catholic Dames stopped paying attention, overwhelmed by the heat. Rebeca Asís unfolded her fan again, and then Father Ángel discovered the source of her fragrance. The sandalwood odor crystallized in the drowsiness of the room. The priest drew the handkerchief out of his sleeve and brought it to his nose so as not to sneeze.

"At the same time," he continued, "our church is the

poorest in the apostolic prefecture. The bells are cracked and the naves are full of mice, because my life has been used up imposing moral standards and good habits."

He unbuttoned his collar. "Any young man can do the rude labor," he said, standing up. "On the other hand, one needs the tenacity of many years and age-old experience to rebuild morals." Rebeca Asís raised her transparent hand, with its wedding band topped by a ring with emeralds.

"For that very reason," she said. "We thought that with these lampoons, all your work might be lost."

The only woman who had remained silent until then took advantage of the pause to intervene.

"Besides, we thought that the country is recuperating and that this present calamity might cause trouble."

Father Ángel took a fan out of the closet and began to fan himself parsimoniously.

"One thing has nothing to do with the other," he said. "We've gone through a difficult political moment, but family morals have been maintained intact."

He stood up before the three women. "Within a few years I shall go tell the apostolic prefecture: I leave you that exemplary town. Now all that's needed is for you to send a young and active fellow to build the best church in the prefecture."

He gave a languid bow and exclaimed:

"Then I will go to die in peace in the courtyard of my ancestors."

The Dames protested. Adalgisa Montoya expressed the general thought:

"This is like your own town, Father. And we want you to stay here until the last moment."

"If it's a question of building a new church," Rebeca Asís said, "we can start the campaign tomorrow."

"All in good time," Father Ángel replied.

Then, in a different tone, he added: "As for now, I don't want to grow old at the head of any parish. I don't want to happen to me what happened to meek Antonio Isabel del Santísimo Sacramento del Altar Castañeda y Montero, who informed the bishop that a rain of dead birds was falling in his parish. The investigator sent by the bishop found him in the main square, playing cops and robbers with the children."

The Dames expressed their perplexity.

"Who was he?"

"The curate who succeeded me in Macondo," Father Ángel said. "He was one hundred years old."

*T*HE WINTER, whose inclemency had been foreseen since the last days of September, implanted its rigor that weekend. The mayor spent Sunday chewing analgesic tablets in his hammock while the river overflowed its banks and damaged the lower parts of town.

During the first letup in the rain, on Monday at dawn, the town needed several hours to recover. The poolroom and the barbershop opened early, but most of the houses remained shut up until eleven o'clock. Mr. Carmichael was the first to have the opportunity to shudder at the spectacle of men carrying their houses to higher ground. Bustling groups had dug up pilings and were transferring intact the fragile habitations of wattle walls and palm roofs.

Taking refuge under the eaves of the barbershop, his umbrella open, Mr. Carmichael was contemplating the laborious maneuvers when the barber drew him out of his abstraction.

"They should have waited for it to clear," the barber said.

"It won't clear for two days," said Mr. Carmichael, and he shut his umbrella. "My corns tell me."

The men carrying the houses, sunk in the mud up to their ankles, passed by, bumping into the walls of the barber-shop. Mr. Carmichael saw the tumble-down insides through the window, a bedroom completely despoiled of its intimacy, and he felt invaded by a sense of disaster.

It seemed like six in the morning, but his stomach told him that it was going on twelve. Moisés the Syrian invited him to sit in his shop until the rain passed. Mr. Carmichael reiterated his prediction that it wouldn't clear for the next forty-eight hours. He hesitated before leaping onto the boardwalk of the next building. A group of boys who were playing war threw a mud ball that splattered on the wall a few feet from his newly pressed pants. Elías the Syrian came out of his shop with a broom in his hand, threatening the boys in an algebra of Arabic and Castilian.

The boys leaped merrily.

"Dumb Turk, go to work."

Mr. Carmichael saw that his clothing was intact. Then he closed his umbrella and went into the barbershop, directly to the chair.

"I always said that you were a prudent man," the barber said.

He tied a towel around his neck. Mr. Carmichael breathed in the smell of lavender water, which produced the same upset in him as the glacial vapors of the dentist's office. The barber began by trimming the curly hair on the back of his neck. Impatient, Mr. Carmichael looked around for something to read.

"Don't you have any newspapers?"

The barber answered without pausing at his work.

"The only newspapers left in the country are the official ones and they won't enter this establishment as long as I'm alive."

Mr. Carmichael satisfied himself with contemplating his wing-tipped shoes until the barber asked about the widow Montiel. He'd come from her place. He'd been the administrator of her affairs ever since the death of Don Chepe Montiel, whose bookkeeper he'd been for many years.

"She's there," he said.

"A person goes on killing himself," the barber said as if talking to himself, "and there she is all alone with a piece of land you couldn't cross in five days on horseback. She must own some ten towns."

"Three," Mr. Carmichael said. And he added with conviction: "She's the finest woman in all the world."

The barber went over to the counter to clean the comb. Mr. Carmichael saw his goat face reflected in the mirror and once more understood why he didn't respect him. The barber spoke, looking at the image.

"A fine business: my party gets in power, the police threaten my political opponents with death, and I buy up their land and livestock at a price I set myself."

Mr. Carmichael lowered his head. The barber applied himself to cutting his hair again. "When the elections are over," he concluded, "I own three towns, I've got no competition, and along the way I've managed to get the upper hand even if the government changes. All I can say is: It's the best business there is; even better than counterfeiting."

"José Montiel was rich long before the political troubles started," Mr. Carmichael said.

"Sitting in his drawers by the door of a rice bin," the barber said. "The story goes that he put on his first pair of shoes at the age of nine."

"And even if that were so," Mr. Carmichael admitted,

"the widow had nothing to do with Montiel's business."

"But she played the dummy," the barber said.

Mr. Carmichael raised his head. He loosened the towel around his neck to let the circulation through. "That's why I've always preferred that my wife cut my hair," he protested. "She doesn't charge me anything, and on top of that, she doesn't talk politics." The barber pushed his head forward and continued working in silence. Sometimes he clicked his scissors in the air to let off an excess of virtuosity. Mr. Carmichael heard shouts from the street. He looked in the mirror: children and women were passing by the door with the furniture and utensils from the houses that were being carried. He commented with rancor:

"Misfortune is eating at us, and you people still with your political hatreds. The persecution's been over for a year and they still talk about the same thing."

"The state of abandonment we're in is persecution too," the barber said.

"But they don't beat us up," Mr. Carmichael said.

"Abandoning us to God's mercy is another way of beating us up."

Mr. Carmichael became exasperated.

"That's newspaper talk," he said.

The barber remained silent. He worked up some lather in a mug and anointed the back of Mr. Carmichael's neck with the brush. "It's just that a person is busting with talk," he apologized. "It isn't every day that we get an impartial man."

"No man can help being impartial with eleven children to feed," Mr. Carmichael said.

"Agreed," said the barber.

He made the razor sing on the palm of his hand. He shaved the neck in silence, cleaning off the soap on his fingers and then cleaning his fingers on his pants. Finally he rubbed a piece of alum on the back of the neck. He finished in silence.

While he was buttoning up his collar, Mr. Carmichael saw the notice nailed to the back wall: *Talking Politics Prohibited.* He brushed the pieces of hair from his shoulders, hung his umbrella over his arm, and pointing to the notice, asked:

"Why don't you take it down?"

"It doesn't apply to you," the barber said. "We've already agreed that you're an impartial man."

Mr. Carmichael didn't hesitate that time to leap onto the boardwalk. The barber watched him until he turned the corner, and then he grew ecstatic over the roiled and threatening river. It had stopped raining, but a heavy cloud hung motionless over the town. A short time before one o'clock Moisés the Syrian came in, lamenting that the hair was falling out of his skull and yet, on the other hand, it was growing on the back of his neck with extraordinary rapidity.

The Syrian had his hair cut every Monday. Ordinarily he would lower his head with a kind of fatalism and snore in Arabic while the barber talked to himself out loud. That Monday, however, he awoke with a start at the first question.

"Do you know who was just here?"

"Carmichael," the Syrian said.

"Rotten old black Carmichael," the barber confirmed as if he had spelled out the phrase. "I detest that kind of man."

"Carmichael isn't a man," Moisés the Syrian said. "He hasn't bought a pair of shoes in more than three years. But in politics he does what has to be done: he keeps books with his eyes closed."

He settled his beard on his chin to snore again, but the barber planted himself in front of him with his arms folded, saying: "Tell me one thing, you shitty Turk: When all's said and done, whose side are you on?" The Syrian answered, unflustered:

"Mine."

"You're wrong," the barber said. "You ought to at least keep in mind the four ribs they broke on your fellow countryman Elías's son on orders from Don Chepe Montiel."

"Elías is all upset that his son turned out to be a politician," the Syrian said. "But now the boy's having a grand time dancing in Brazil and Chepe Montiel is dead."

Before leaving the room which was in disorder from his long nights of suffering, the mayor shaved the right side of his face, leaving the other side with its week-old beard. Then he put on a clean uniform, his patent leather boots, and went down to eat in the hotel, taking advantage of the pause in the rain.

There was no one in the dining room. The mayor made his way through the small tables for four and occupied the most discreet spot in the back of the room.

"Masks," he called.

He was answered by a very young girl with a short tight dress and breasts like stones. The mayor ordered lunch without looking at her. On her way back to the kitchen the girl turned on the radio placed on a shelf at the end of the dining room. A news bulletin came on, with quotations from a speech given the night before by the president of the republic, and then a list of new items prohibited for import. The heat grew more intense as the announcer's voice filled the space. When the girl returned with the soup, the mayor was trying to check the heat by fanning himself with his cap.

"The radio makes me sweat too," the girl said.

The mayor began to drink his soup. He'd always thought that that solitary hotel, sustained by occasional traveling salesmen, was a different place from the rest of the town.

Actually, it antedated the town. On its run-down wooden balcony, merchants who came from the interior to buy the rice harvest used to spend the night playing cards and waiting for the coolness of dawn in order to be able to sleep. Colonel Aureliano Buendía himself, on his way to Macondo to draw up the terms of surrender in the last civil war, had slept on that balcony one night during a time when there weren't any towns for many leagues around. It was the same building then, with wooden walls and a zinc roof, with the same dining room and the same cardboard partitions, except with no electricity or sanitary services. An old traveling salesman recounted that until the turn of the century there had been a collection of masks hanging in the dining room at the disposal of the customers, and that the masked guests took care of their needs in the courtyard in full view of everyone.

The mayor had to unbutton his collar in order to finish the soup. After the news bulletin there was a record with rhyming commercials. Then a sentimental bolero. A man with a mentholated voice, dying with love, has decided to travel around the world in pursuit of a woman. The mayor gave his attention to the room while he waited for the rest of his meal; he even saw two children with two chairs and a rocker pass in front of the hotel. Behind came two women and a man with pots and tubs and the rest of the furniture.

He went to the door, shouting:

"Where did you steal that junk?"

The women stopped. The man explained to him that they were transferring their house to higher ground. The mayor asked where they'd taken it and the man pointed toward the south with his hat:

"Up there, to a lot that Don Sabas rented us for thirty pesos."

The mayor examined the furniture. A rocker that was

falling apart at the joints, broken pots: poor people's things. He reflected for an instant. Finally he said:

"Take those houses and all your goods to the vacant lot beside the cemetery."

The man became confused.

"It's town land and it won't cost you anything," the mayor said. "The town government gives it to you."

Then, turning to the women, he added: "And tell Don Sabas that I send him a message not to be a highway robber."

He finished his lunch without tasting the food. Then he lighted a cigarette. He lighted another with the butt and was thoughtful for a long time, resting his elbows on the table while the radio ground out sentimental boleros.

"What are you thinking about?" the girl asked, clearing away the empty plates.

The mayor didn't blink.

"Those poor people."

He put on his cap and crossed the room. Turning around from the door, he said:

"We've got to make this town a decent sort of mess."

A bloody dogfight interrupted his passage as he turned the corner. He saw a knot of backs and legs in a whirlwind of howls and then bared teeth and one dog dragging a limb, its tail between its legs. The mayor stepped to one side and went along the boardwalk toward the police barracks.

A woman was shouting in the lockup, while the guard was sleeping his siesta lying face down on a cot. The mayor kicked the leg of the cot. The guard awoke with a leap.

"Who's she?" the mayor asked.

The guard came to attention.

"The woman who was putting up the lampoons."

The mayor broke out in curses against his subordinates. He wanted to know who'd brought the woman there and under whose orders they'd put her in the lockup. The policemen gave an extravagant explanation.

"When did you lock her up?"

They had jailed her Saturday night.

"Well, she comes out and one of you goes in," the mayor shouted. "That woman was asleep in the lockup and the whole town woke up papered."

As soon as the heavy iron door was opened, a mature woman with pronounced bones and a bumptious bun held in place by a comb came shouting out of the cell.

"You can go to hell," she said to the mayor.

The woman loosened the bun, shook her long, abundant hair several times, and went down the stairs like a stampede, shouting: "Whore, whore." The mayor leaned over the railing and shouted with all the power of his voice, as if not only the woman and his men but the whole town were meant to hear him:

"And stop fucking me up with those damned papers."

Although the drizzle persisted, Father Ángel went out to take his afternoon walk. It was still early for his appointment with the mayor, so he went to the flooded part of town. All he found was the corpse of a cat floating among the flowers.

While he was coming back, the afternoon began to dry out. It was getting intense and bright. A barge covered with tar paper was coming down the thick and motionless river. From a half-collapsed house a child ran out, shouting that he'd found the sea inside a shell. Father Ángel put the shell to his ear. Indeed, there was the sea.

Judge Arcadio's wife was sitting by the door of their house as if in ecstasy, her arms folded over her stomach and her eyes fixed on the barge. Three houses beyond, the shops began, the showcases with their trinkets and the impassive Syrians sitting in the doorways. The afternoon was dying with intense pink clouds and the uproar of parrots and monkeys on the opposite shore.

The houses began to open up. Under the dirty almond trees on the square, around the refreshment carts, or on the worn granite benches in the flower beds, the men were gathering to chat. Father Ángel thought that every afternoon at that instant the town went through the miracle of transfiguration.

"Father, do you remember the concentration camp prisoners?"

Father Ángel didn't see Dr. Giraldo, but he pictured him smiling behind the screened window. In all honesty he didn't remember the photographs, but he was sure he'd seen them at one time or another.

"Go into the waiting room," the doctor said.

Father Ángel pushed open the screen door. Stretched out on a mattress was a child of indefinite sex, nothing but bones, covered all over by yellowed skin. Two men and a woman were waiting, sitting by the partition. The priest didn't smell any odor, but he thought that that creature should have been giving off an intense stench.

"Who is it?" he asked.

"My son," the woman answered. And she added, as if excusing herself, "For two years he's been shitting a little blood."

The patient made his eyes turn toward the door without moving his head. The priest felt a terrified pity.

"And what have you done for him?" he asked.

"We've been giving him green bananas for a long time," the woman said, "but he hasn't wanted to take them, even though they're nice and binding."

"You have to bring him to confession," the priest said.

But he said it without conviction. He closed the door

carefully and scratched on the window screen with a fingernail, putting his face close in order to see the doctor inside. Dr. Giraldo was grinding something in a mortar.

"What's he got?" the priest asked.

"I still haven't examined him," the doctor answered. And he commented thoughtfully, "There are things that happen to people by God's will, Father."

Father Ángel let the comment pass.

"None of the dead people I've seen in my life seemed as dead as that poor boy," he said.

He took his leave. There were no vessels at the dock. It was beginning to get dark. Father Ángel understood that his state of mind had changed with the sight of the sick boy. Realizing that he was late for his appointment, he walked faster toward the police barracks.

The mayor was collapsed in a folding chair with his head in his hands.

"Good evening," the priest said slowly.

The mayor raised his head and the priest shuddered at the eyes reddened by desperation. He had one cheek cool and newly shaved, but the other was a swampy tangle of an unguent the color of ashes. He exclaimed in a dull moan:

"Father, I'm going to shoot myself."

Father Ángel felt a certain consternation.

"You're getting drunk from so many aspirins," he said.

The mayor shuffled over to the wall, and clutching his head in both hands, he pounded it violently against the boards. The priest had never witnessed such pain.

"Take two more pills," he said, consciously proposing a remedy for his own confusion. "Two more won't kill you."

Not only was that really true, but he was fully aware that he was awkward facing human pain. He looked for the analgesics in the naked space of the room. Up against the walls there were half a dozen leather stools, a glass cabinet stuffed with dusty papers, and a lithograph of the president of the republic hanging from a nail. The only trace of the analgesics was the cellophane wrappings strewn on the floor.

"Where are they?" he said desperately.

"They don't have any more effect on me," the mayor said.

The curate went over to him, repeating: "Tell me where they are." The mayor gave a violent twitch and Father Ángel saw an enormous and monstrous face a few inches from his eyes.

"God damn it," the mayor shouted. "I already said they don't do me a fucking bit of good."

He lifted a stool above his head and flung it with all the might of his desperation against the glass case. Father Ángel only understood what had happened after the instantaneous drizzle of glass, when the mayor began to rise up like a serene apparition in the midst of the cloud of dust. At that moment there was a perfect silence.

"Lieutenant," the priest murmured.

In the door to the porch stood the policemen with their rifles at the ready. The mayor looked at them without seeing them, breathing like a cat, and they lowered their rifles but remained motionless beside the door. Father Ángel led the mayor by the arm to the folding chair.

"Where are the analgesics?" he insisted.

The mayor closed his eyes and threw his head back. "I'm not taking any more of that junk," he said. "My ears are buzzing and the bones of my skull are going to sleep on me." During a brief respite in the pain, he turned his head to the priest and asked:

"Did you talk to the tooth-puller?"

The priest said yes silently. From the expression that

followed that reply the mayor learned the results of the interview.

"Why don't you talk to Dr. Giraldo?" the priest proposed. "There are doctors who pull teeth."

The mayor delayed in answering. "He'll probably say he hasn't got any forceps," he said. And he added:

"It's a plot."

He took advantage of the respite to rest from that implacable afternoon. When he opened his eyes the room was in shadows. He said, without seeing Father Ángel:

"You came about César Montero."

He didn't hear any answer. "With this pain I haven't been able to do anything," he went on. He got up to turn on the light and the first wave of mosquitoes came in through the balcony. Father Ángel was surprised at the hour.

"Time is passing," he said.

"He has to be sent off on Wednesday in any case," the mayor said. "Tomorrow arrange what has to be arranged and confess him in the afternoon."

"What time?"

"Four o'clock."

"Even if it's raining?"

In a single look, the mayor liberated all the impatience repressed during two weeks of suffering.

"Even if the world is coming to an end, Father."

The pain had become invulnerable to the analgesics. The mayor hung the hammock on the balcony of his room, trying to sleep in the coolness of early evening. But before eight o'clock he succumbed again to desperation and went down into the square, which was in a lethargy from a dense wave of heat.

After roaming about the area without finding the inspiration he needed to rise above the pain, he went into the movie theater. It was a mistake. The buzz of the warplanes increased the intensity of the pain. He left the theater before intermission and got to the pharmacy just as Don Lalo Moscote was getting ready to close the doors.

"Give me the strongest thing you've got for a toothache."

The druggist examined the cheek with a look of stupor. Then he went to the rear of the establishment, past a double row of cabinets with glass doors which were completely filled with porcelain vials, each with the name of a product written in blue letters. On looking at him from behind, the mayor understood that that man with a chubby and pink neck might be living an instant of happiness. He knew him. He was installed in two rooms behind the store and his wife, a very fat woman, had been paralyzed for many years.

Don Lalo Moscote came back to the counter with a vial that had no label, which, on being opened, exhaled a vapor of sweet herbs.

"What's that?"

The druggist sank his fingers into the dried seeds in the vial. "Pepper cress," he said. "Chew it well and swallow the juice slowly: there's nothing better for rheumatism." He threw several seeds into the palm of his hand and said, looking at the mayor over his glasses:

"Open your mouth."

The mayor drew back. He turned the vial around to make sure that nothing was written on it, and returned his look to the pharmacist.

"Give me something foreign," he said.

"This is better than anything foreign," Don Lalo Moscote said. "It's guaranteed by three thousand years of popular wisdom."

He began to wrap up the seeds in a piece of newspaper. He didn't look like the head of a family. He looked like a maternal uncle, wrapping up the pepper cress with the loving care one devotes to making little paper birds for children. When he raised his head he'd begun to smile.

"Why don't you have it pulled?"

The mayor didn't answer. He paid with a bill and left the pharmacy without waiting for his change.

Past midnight he was still twisting in his hammock without daring to chew the seeds. Around eleven o'clock, at the high point of the heat, a cloudburst had fallen that had broken up into a light drizzle. Worn out by the fever, trembling in a sticky and icy sweat, the mayor, lying face down in the hammock, opened his mouth and began to pray mentally. He prayed deeply, his muscles tense in the final spasm, but aware that the more he struggled to make contact with God, the greater the force of the pain to push him in the opposite direction. Then he put on his boots, and his raincoat over his pajamas, and went to the police barracks.

He burst in shouting. Tangled in a mangrove of reality and nightmare, the policemen stumbled in the hallway, looking for their weapons in the darkness. When the lights went on they were half dressed, awaiting orders.

"González, Rovira, Peralta," the mayor shouted.

The three named separated from the group and surrounded the lieutenant. There was no visible reason to justify the selection: they were three ordinary half-breeds. One of them, with infantile features, shaven head, was wearing a flannel undershirt. The other two were wearing the same undershirt under unbuttoned tunics.

They didn't receive precise orders. Leaping down the stairs four steps at a time behind the mayor, they left the barracks in Indian file. They crossed the street without worrying about the drizzle and stopped in front of the dentist's office. With two quick charges they battered down the door with their rifle butts. They were already inside the house when the lights in the vestibule went on. A small bald man with veins showing through his skin appeared in his shorts at the rear door, trying to put on his bathrobe. At the first instant he remained paralyzed with one arm up and his mouth open, as in the flash of a photograph. Then he gave a leap backward and bumped into his wife, who was coming out of the bedroom in her nightgown.

"Don't move," the lieutenant shouted.

The woman said: "Oh!" with her hands over her mouth, and went back to the bedroom. The dentist went toward the vestibule, tying the cord on his bathrobe, and only then did he make out the three policemen who were pointing their rifles at him, and the mayor, water dripping from all over his body, tranquil, his hands in the pockets of his raincoat.

"If the lady leaves her room they have orders to shoot her," the lieutenant said.

The dentist grasped the doorknob, saying to the inside: "You heard, girl," and he meticulously closed the bedroom door. Then he walked to the dental office, observed past the faded wicker furniture by the smoky eyes of the rifle barrels. Two policemen went ahead of him to the door of the office. One turned on the light; the other went directly to the worktable and took a revolver out of the drawer.

"There must be another," the mayor said.

He had entered last, behind the dentist. The two policemen made a quick and conscientious search while the third guarded the door. They dumped the instrument box onto the worktable, scattered plaster molds, unfinished false teeth, loose teeth, and gold caps on the floor. They emptied the porcelain vials that were in the cabinet and, making quick stabs with their bayonets, gutted the oilcloth cushion on the dentist's chair and the spring cushion on the revolving chair.

"It's a long-barreled thirty-eight," the mayor specified.

He scrutinized the dentist. "It would be better if you said outright where it is," he told him. "We didn't come prepared to tear the house apart." Behind his gold-framed glasses the dentist's dull and narrow eyes revealed nothing.

"There's no hurry on my part," he replied in a relaxed way. "If you feel like it, you can go right on tearing it apart."

The mayor reflected. After once more examining the small room made of unplaned planks, he went over to the chair, giving sharp commands to his men. He stationed one by the street door, another at the entrance to the office, and the third by the window. When he was settled in the chair, only then unbuttoning his soaked raincoat, he felt surrounded by cold steel. He breathed in deeply of the air, rarefied by creosote, and rested his skull against the headrest, trying to control his breathing. The dentist picked some instruments up off the floor and put them in a pot to boil.

He remained with his back to the mayor, contemplating the blue flame of the alcohol lamp with the same expression that he must have had when he was alone in the office. When the water was boiling, he wrapped the handle of the pot in a piece of paper and carried it over to the chair. His way was blocked by a policeman. The dentist lowered the pot, to look at the mayor over the steam, and said:

"Order this assassin to go someplace where he won't be in the way."

On a signal from the mayor, the policeman moved away from the window in order to give free access to the chair. He pulled a chair against the wall and sat down with his legs apart, the rifle across his thighs, without relaxing his vigilance. The dentist turned on the lamp. Dazzled by the sudden light, the mayor closed his eyes and opened his mouth. The pain had stopped.

The dentist located the sick molar, using his index finger to push aside the inflamed cheek and adjusting the movable lamp with the other hand, completely insensible to the patient's anxious breathing. Then he rolled his sleeve up to the elbow and got ready to pull the tooth.

The mayor grabbed him by the wrist.

"Anesthesia," he said.

Their eyes met for the first time.

"You people kill without anesthesia," the dentist said softly.

The mayor didn't notice any effort to free itself in the hand that was holding the forceps. "Bring the vials," he said. The policeman stationed in the corner moved his rifle barrel in their direction and they both heard the sound of the rifle as it was cocked from the chair.

"Suppose there isn't any," the dentist said.

The mayor let go of his wrist. "There has to be," he replied, examining the things scattered on the floor with disconsolate interest. The dentist watched him with sympathetic attention. Then he pushed him back against the headrest and, showing signs of impatience for the first time, said:

"Don't be a fool, Lieutenant. With an abscess like that, no anesthesia will be any good."

Later, having suffered the most terrible moment of his life, the mayor relaxed the tension of his muscles, and remained in the chair exhausted as the dark designs painted by the dampness on the cardboard ceiling fastened themselves in his memory, to remain until the day he died. He heard the dentist busying himself at the washstand. He heard him putting the desk drawers in order and picking up some of the objects from the floor.

"Rovira," the mayor called. "Tell González to come in and you two pick up the things off the floor until the place is the way you found it."

The policemen did so. The dentist picked up some cotton with his pincers, soaked it in an iron-colored liquid, and covered the hole. The mayor had a feeling of burning on the surface. After the dentist had closed his mouth he continued with his gaze on the ceiling, hanging on the sound of the policemen as they tried to reconstruct from memory the meticulous order of the office. It struck two in the belfry. A curlew, a minute behind, repeated the hour in the murmur of the drizzle. A moment later, knowing that they had finished, the mayor gave a sign indicating that his men should return to the barracks.

The dentist had remained beside the chair all the while. When the policemen had left, he took the cotton out of the gum. Then he explored the inside of the mouth with the lamp, adjusted the jaws again, and took the light away. Everything was over. In the hot little room all that remained then was that strange uneasiness known to sweepers in a theater after the last actor has left.

"Ingrate," the mayor said.

The dentist put his hands in the pockets of his robe and took a step backward to let him pass. "There were orders to level the house," the mayor went on, searching for him with his eyes behind the circle of light. "There were precise instructions to *find* weapons and ammunition and documents with the details of a nation-wide conspiracy." He fixed his still damp eyes on the dentist and added: "I thought that I was doing the right thing by disobeying that order, but I was wrong. Things have changed now. The opposition has guarantes and everybody is living in peace, and still you go on thinking like a conspirator." The dentist dried the cushion of the chair with his sleeve and turned it over to the side that hadn't been ruined.

"Your attitude is harmful to the town," the mayor went on, pointing to the cushion, without paying any attention to the thoughtful look the dentist was giving his cheek. "Now it's up to the town government to pay for all this mess, and the street door besides. A whole lot of money, all because of your stubbornness."

"Rinse your mouth out with fenugreek water," the dentist said.

*J*UDGE ARCADIO consulted the dictionary at the telegraph office because his was missing a few letters. It didn't solve anything as he looked up *pasquín,* the word for lampoon: *name of a shoemaker in Rome famous for the satires he wrote against everybody* and other unimportant facts. By the same historic token, he thought, an anonymous insult placed on the door of a house could just as well be called a *marforio.* He wasn't entirely disappointed. During the two minutes he had spent in that consultation, for the first time in many years he had felt the comfort of a duty fulfilled.

The telegrapher saw him put the dictionary back on the shelf among the forgotten compilations of ordinances and decrees concerning the postal and telegraphic service, and cut off the transmission of a message with an energetic signal. Then he came over, shuffling the cards, ready to repeat the latest popular trick: guessing the three cards.

But Judge Arcadio paid no attention to him. "I'm very busy now," he apologized, and went out into the roasting street, pursued by the confused certainty that it was only eleven o'clock and that Tuesday still had a lot of hours left for him to use up.

In his office the mayor was waiting for him with a moral problem. As a result of the last elections, the police had confiscated and destroyed the electoral documents of the opposition party. The majority of the inhabitants of the town now lacked any means of identification.

"Those people moving their houses," the mayor concluded with his arms open, "don't even know what their names are."

Judge Arcadio could understand that there was a sincere affliction behind those open arms. But the mayor's problem was simple: all he had to do was ask for the appointment of a civil registrar. The secretary simplified the solution even further:

"All that's necessary is to send for him," he said. "He was already appointed over a year ago."

The mayor remembered. Months before, when they communicated to him the appointment of a civil registrar, he'd made a long-distance phone call to ask how he should receive him, and they'd answered: "With bullets." Now the orders that came were different. He turned to the secretary with his hands in his pockets, and told him:

"Write the letter."

The clack of the typewriter produced a dynamic atmosphere in the office, which echoed in Judge Arcadio's consciousness. He found himself empty. He took a crumpled cigarette out of his shirt pocket and rolled it between the palms of his hands before lighting it. Then he threw his chair back to the limit of its springs and in that posture he was startled by the definite certainty that he was living out a minute of his life.

He put the phrase together before he said it:

"If I were in your place, I would also appoint a deputy of the public ministry."

Contrary to what he had hoped, the mayor didn't answer right away. He looked at his watch, but didn't see the time. He settled on the evidence that it was still a long time until lunch. When he spoke, he did so without enthusiasm: he wasn't familiar with the procedure for appointing a deputy of the public ministry.

"The deputy used to be named by the town council," Judge Arcadio explained. "Since there's no council now, the government by state of siege authorizes you to name one."

The mayor listened, while he signed the letter without reading it. Then he made an enthusiastic comment, but the secretary had an observation of an ethical nature to make concerning the procedure recommended by his superior. Judge Arcadio insisted: it was an emergency procedure under an emergency regime.

"I like the sound of it," the mayor said.

He took off his cap to fan himself and Judge Arcadio noticed the circular mark printed on his forehead. From the way in which he was fanning himself, he knew that the mayor hadn't finished thinking. He knocked the ash off his cigarette with the long, curved nail of his pinky and waited.

"Can you think of a candidate?" the mayor asked.

It was obvious that he was addressing the secretary.

"A candidate," the judge repeated, closing his eyes.

"If I were in your place, I'd name an honest man," the secretary said.

The judge caught the impertinence. "That's more than

obvious," he said, and looked alternately at the two men.

"For example," the mayor said.

"I can't think of anyone right now," said the judge, thoughtful.

The mayor went to the door. "Think about it," he said. "When we get out of the mess of the floods we'll take up the mess of the deputy." The secretary sat hanging over his typewriter until he no longer heard the mayor's heels.

"He's crazy," he said then. "A year and a half ago they busted the head of the deputy with rifle butts and now he's looking for a candidate to give the job to."

Judge Arcadio leaped to his feet.

"I'm leaving," he said. "I don't want you to spoil my lunch with your horror stories."

He went out of the office. There was an ominous element in the composition of noontime. The secretary, with his sensitivity to superstition, noticed it. When he put on the padlock he felt that he was performing a forbidden act. He fled. At the door of the telegraph office he caught up with Judge Arcadio, who was interested in seeing if the card trick was in any way applicable to a game of poker. The telegrapher refused to reveal the secret. He limited himself to repeating the trick indefinitely in order to give Judge Arcadio a chance to discover the clue. The secretary also observed the maneuver. Finally he reached a conclusion. Judge Arcadio, on the other hand, didn't even look at the three cards. He knew that they were the same ones he'd picked at random and that the telegrapher was giving them back to him without having seen them.

"It's a matter of magic," the telegrapher said.

Judge Arcadio was only thinking then of the chore of crossing the street. When he resigned himself to walking, he grabbed the secretary by the arm and obliged him to dive with him into the melted-glass atmosphere. They emerged onto the shaded sidewalk. Then the secretary explained to him the key to the trick. It was so simple that Judge Arcadio felt offended.

They walked in silence for a spell.

"Naturally," the judge said suddenly with a gratuitous rancor, "you didn't check the information out."

The secretary hesitated for an instant, searching for the meaning of the sentence.

"It's very hard," he finally said. "Most of the lampoons are torn down before dawn."

"That's another trick I don't understand," Judge Arcadio said. "I'd never lose any sleep over a lampoon that nobody's read."

"That's just it," the secretary said, stopping because he'd reached his house. "It isn't the lampoons that won't let people sleep; it's fear of the lampoons."

In spite of its being incomplete, Judge Arcadio wanted to know what information the secretary had gathered. He enumerated the cases, with names and dates: eleven in seven days. There was no connection among the eleven names. Those who'd seen the lampoons agreed that they'd been written with a brush in blue ink and in printed letters, with capitals and small letters mixed up as if written by a child. The spelling was so absurd that the mistakes looked deliberate. They revealed no secrets: there was nothing said in them that hadn't been in the public domain for some time. He'd made all the conjectures that were possible when Moisés the Syrian called to him from his shop.

"Have you got a peso?"

Judge Arcadio didn't understand. But he turned his pockets inside out: twenty-five centavos and an American coin that he'd kept as a good luck charm ever since his university days. Moisés the Syrian took the twenty-five centavos.

"Take whatever you want and pay me whenever you want to," he said. He made the coins tinkle in the empty cash drawer. "I don't want twelve o'clock to strike on me without having heard God's name."

So at the stroke of twelve Judge Arcadio entered his house laden with gifts for his wife. He sat on the bed to change his shoes while she wrapped up her body in a swathe of printed silk. She pictured her appearance in the new dress after the birth. She gave her husband a kiss on the nose. He tried to avoid her, but she fell on top of him across the bed. They remained motionless. Judge Arcadio ran his hand over her back, feeling the warmth of the voluminous belly, even as he perceived the palpitation of her kidneys.

She raised her head. Murmured with her teeth tight:

"Wait and I'll go close the door."

The mayor waited until the last house was set up. In twenty hours they'd built a whole street, wide and bare, which ended abruptly at the cemetery wall. After helping place the furniture, working shoulder to shoulder with the owners, the mayor, smothering, entered the nearest kitchen. Soup was boiling on a stove improvised from stones on the ground. He took the lid off the clay pot and breathed in the vapor for a moment. From across the stove a thin woman with large, peaceful eyes was observing him silently.

"Lunchtime," the mayor said.

The woman didn't answer. Without being invited, the mayor served himself a plate of soup. Then the woman went into the bedroom to get a chair and put it by the table for the mayor to sit on. While he was having his soup, he examined the yard with a kind of reverent terror. Yesterday it had been a barren vacant lot. Now there was clothing hung to dry and two pigs were wallowing in the mud.

"You can even plant something," he said.

Without raising her head, the woman answered: "The pigs will eat it." Then, in the same plate, she served a piece of stewed meat, two slices of cassava, and half a plantain and took it to the table. In an obvious way, into that act of generosity she put all the indifference she was capable of. The mayor, smiling, sought the woman's eyes with his.

"There's enough for all," he said.

"May God give you indigestion," the woman said without looking at him.

He let the bad wish pass. He dedicated himself entirely to his lunch, not concerned with the stream of sweat pouring down his neck. When he had finished, the woman took the empty plate, still not looking at him.

"How long are you people going to go on like this?" the mayor asked.

The woman spoke without changing her apathetic expression.

"Until you people bring the dead you killed back to life."

"It's different now," the mayor explained. "The new government is concerned with the well-being of its citizens. You people, on the other hand—"

The woman interrupted him.

"You're the same people with the same—"

"A district like this, built in twenty-four hours, was something you never saw before," the mayor insisted. "We're trying to build a decent town."

The woman took the clean clothes off the line and carried them into the bedroom. The mayor followed her with his eyes until he heard the answer:

"This was a decent town before you people came."

He didn't wait for any coffee. "Ingrates," he said. "We're giving you land and you still complain." The woman didn't answer. But when the mayor crossed the kitchen on his way to the street, she muttered, leaning over the stove:

"It'll be worse here. But we'll remember you people from the dead out back there."

The mayor tried to sleep a siesta while the launches were arriving. But he couldn't fight the heat. The swelling on his cheek had begun to subside. Still, he didn't feel well. He followed the imperceptible course of the river for two hours, listening to the buzz of a harvest fly inside the room. He didn't think about anything.

When he heard the motors of the launches he got undressed, dried his sweat with a towel, and changed his uniform. Then he hunted for the harvest fly, grabbed it between his thumb and forefinger, and went into the street. Out of the crowd waiting for the launches came a clean, well-dressed child who cut off his path with a plastic submachine gun. The mayor gave him the harvest fly.

A moment later, sitting in Moisés the Syrian's store, he watched the docking maneuvers of the launches. The port had been boiling for ten minutes. The mayor felt a heaviness in his stomach and a touch of headache, and he remembered the woman's bad wishes. Then he calmed down and watched the passengers coming down the wooden gangplank, stretching their muscles after eight hours of immobility.

"The same mess," he said.

Moisés the Syrian brought him to the realization of something new: a circus was coming. The mayor noticed that it was true, even though he couldn't say why. Maybe because of the poles and colored cloth all piled up on the roof of the launch, and because of two women completely alike wrapped in identical flowered dresses, like a single person repeated.

"At least a circus is coming," he murmured.

Moisés the Syrian talked about wild animals and jugglers.

But the mayor thought about the circus in a different way. With his legs stretched out, he looked at the tips of his boots.

"The town's making progress," he said.

Moisés the Syrian stopped fanning himself. "Do you know how much I've sold today?" he asked. The mayor didn't venture any guess, but waited for the answer.

"Twenty-five centavos' worth," the Syrian said.

At that instant the mayor saw the telegrapher opening the mailbag to give Dr. Giraldo his letters. He called him over. The official mail came in a distinct envelope. He broke the seals and realized that they were routine communications and printed sheets with propaganda for the regime. When he finished reading them, the dock had been transformed: boxes of merchandise, crates of chickens, and the enigmatic artifacts of the circus. Dusk was coming on. He stood up, sighing.

"Twenty-five centavos."

"Twenty-five centavos," repeated the Syrian in a firm voice with almost no accent.

Dr. Giraldo watched the unloading of the launches until the end. He was the one who drew the mayor's attention to a vigorous woman of solemn bearing with several sets of bracelets on both arms. She seemed to be waiting for the Messiah under a multicolored parasol. The mayor didn't stop to think about the newcomer.

"She must be the animal tamer," he said.

"In a manner of speaking, you're right," Dr. Giraldo said, biting off his words with his double row of sharpened stones. "It's César Montero's mother-in-law."

The mayor continued on slowly. He looked at his watch: twenty-five to four. At the door of the barracks the guard informed him that Father Ángel had waited for half an hour and would be back at four o'clock.

On the street again, not knowing what to do, he saw the dentist in the window of his office and went over to ask him for a light. The dentist gave it to him, looking at the still swollen cheek.

"I'm fine," the mayor said.

He opened his mouth. The dentist observed:

"There are several cavities to be filled."

The mayor adjusted the revolver at his waist. "I'll be by," he decided. The dentist didn't change his expression.

"Come whenever you want to, to see if my wish to have you die in my house comes true."

The mayor patted him on the shoulder. "It won't," he commented, in a good mood. And he concluded, his arms open:

"My teeth are above party politics."

"So you won't get married?"

Judge Arcadio's wife opened her legs. "No hope at all, Father," she answered. "And even less now that I'm going to have a child." Father Ángel averted his gaze toward the river. A drowned cow, enormous, was coming down along the streams of the current, with several buzzards on top of it.

"But it will be an illegitimate child," he said.

"That doesn't matter," she said. "Arcadio treats me well now. If I make him marry me, then he'll feel tied down and make me pay for it."

She had taken off her clogs and was talking with her knees apart, her toes riding the crossbar of the stool. Her fan was in her lap and her arms were folded over her voluminous belly. "No hope at all, Father," she repeated, because Father Ángel had remained silent. "Don Sabas bought me for two hundred pesos, sucked my juice out in three months, and then threw me into the street without a pin. If Arcadio hadn't taken me in, I would have starved to death." She looked at the priest for the first time:

"Or I would have had to become a whore."

Father Ángel had been insisting for six months.

"You should make him marry you and set up a home," he said. "This way, the way you're living now, not only leaves you in a precarious situation, but it's a bad example for the town."

"It's better to do things frankly," she said. "Others do the same thing but with the lights out. Haven't you read the lampoons?"

"That's gossip," the priest said. "You have to legitimize your situation and put yourself out of the range of gossiping tongues."

"Me?" she said. "I don't have to put myself out of the range of anything because I do everything in broad daylight. The proof of it is that nobody has wasted his time putting any lampoon on my door, and on the other hand, all the decent people on the square have theirs all papered up."

"You're being foolish," the priest said, "but God has given you the good fortune of getting a man who respects you. For that very reason you ought to get married and legalize your home."

"I don't understand those things," she said, "but in any case, just the way I am I've got a place to sleep and I've got plenty to eat."

"What if he abandons you?"

She bit her lip. She smiled enigmatically as she answered:

"He won't abandon me, Father. I know why I can tell you that."

Nor did Father Ángel consider himself defeated that time. He recommended that at least she come to mass. She replied that she would, "one of these days," and the priest continued his walk, waiting for the time to meet with the mayor. One of the Syrians called his attention to the good weather, but he didn't pay any heed. He was interested in the details of the circus that was unloading its anxious wild animals in the bright afternoon. He stayed there until four o'clock.

The mayor was taking leave of the dentist when he saw Father Ángel approaching. "Right on the dot," he said, and shook hands. "Right on the dot, even when it's not raining." Set to climb the steep stairs of the barracks, Father Ángel replied:

"And even if the world is coming to an end."

Two minutes later he was let into César Montero's room.

While the confession was going on the mayor sat in the hall. He thought about the circus, of a woman hanging onto a bit by her teeth, twenty feet in the air, and a man in a blue uniform trimmed with gold beating on a snare drum. Half an hour later Father Ángel left César Montero's room.

"All set?" the mayor asked.

"You people are committing a crime," he said. "That man hasn't eaten for five days. Only his constitution has allowed him to survive."

"That's what he wants," the mayor said tranquilly.

"That's not true," the priest said, putting a serene energy into his voice. "You gave orders that he wasn't to be fed."

The mayor pointed at him.

"Be careful, Father. You're violating the secrets of the confessional."

"That's not part of his confession," the priest said.

The mayor leaped to his feet. "Don't get all worked up," he said, laughing suddenly. "If it worries you so much, we'll fix it up right now." He called a policeman over and gave him an order to have them send some food from the hotel for César Montero. "Have them send over a whole chicken, nice and fat, with a dish of potatoes and a bowl of salad," he said, and added, addressing the priest:

"Everything charged to the town government, Father. So you can see how things have changed."

Father Ángel lowered his head.

"When are you sending him off?"

"The launches leave tomorrow," the mayor said. "If he listens to reason tonight, he'll go tomorrow. He just has to realize that I'm trying to do him a favor."

"A slightly expensive favor," the priest said.

"There's no favor that doesn't cost the person who gets it some money," the mayor said. He fixed his eyes on Father Ángel's clear blue eyes and added:

"I hope you've made him understand all those things."

Father Ángel didn't answer. He went down the stairs and said goodbye from the landing with a dull snort. Then the mayor crossed the hall and went into César Montero's room without knocking.

It was a simple room: a wash basin and an iron bed. César Montero, unshaven, dressed in the same clothing that he had been wearing when he left his house on Tuesday of the week before, was lying on the bed. He didn't even move his eyes when he heard the mayor. "Now that you've settled your accounts with God," the latter said, "there's nothing more just than your doing the same with me." Pulling a chair over to the bed, he straddled it, his chest against the wicker back. César Montero concentrated his attention on the roof beams. He didn't seem worried in spite of the fact that the damage of a long conversation with himself could be seen on the edges of his mouth. "You and I don't have to beat about the bush," he heard the mayor say. "You're leaving tomorrow. If you're lucky, in two or three months a special investigator will arrive. It's up to us to fill him in.

On the launch arriving the following week, you'll return convinced that you did a stupid thing."

He paused, but César Montero remained imperturbable.

"Later on, between courts and lawyers, they'll get at least twenty thousand pesos out of you. Or more should the special investigator see to it that he tells them you're a millionaire."

César Montero turned his head toward him. It was an almost imperceptible movement, but it made the bedsprings squeak.

"All in all," the mayor went on, with the voice of a spiritual adviser, "between twists and paper work, they'll nail you for two years if all goes well for you."

He felt himself being examined from head to toe. When César Montero's gaze reached his eyes, he still hadn't stopped speaking. But he'd changed his tone.

"Everything you've got you owe to me," he said. "There were orders to do you in. There were orders to murder you in ambush and confiscate your livestock so the government would have a way to pay off the enormous expenses of the elections in the whole department. You know that other mayors did it in other towns. Here, on the other hand, we disobeyed the order."

At that moment he perceived the first sign that César Montero was thinking. He opened his legs. His arms leaning on the back of the chair, he responded to the unspoken charge.

"Not one penny of what you paid for your life went to me," he said. "Everything was spent on organizing the elections. Now the new government has decided that there should be peace and guarantees for everybody and I go on being broke on my salary while you're filthy with money. You got yourself a good deal."

César Montero started the laborious process of getting

up. When he was standing, the mayor saw himself: tiny and sad, face to face with a monumental beast. There was a kind of fervor in the look with which he followed him to the window.

"The best deal in your life," he murmured.

The window opened onto the river. César Montero didn't recognize it. He saw himself in a different town, facing a momentary river. "I'm trying to help you," he heard behind him. "We all know that it was a matter of honor, but it'll be hard to prove. You did a stupid thing by tearing up the lampoon." At that instant a strong nauseating smell invaded the room.

"The cow," the mayor said. "It must have washed up somewhere."

César Montero remained at the window, indifferent to the stench of putrefaction. There was nobody on the street. At the dock, three anchored launches, whose crews were hanging up their hammocks for sleep. On the following day, at seven in the morning, the picture would be different: for half an hour the port would be in a turmoil, waiting for the prisoner to embark. César Montero sighed. He put his hands into his pockets and, with a resolute air, but without haste, he summed up his thoughts in two words:

"How much?"

The answer was immediate:

"Five thousand pesos in yearlings."

"Add five more calves," César Montero said, "and send me out this very night, after the movies, on an express launch."

HE LAUNCH blew its whistle, turned around in midstream, and the crowd clustered on the dock and the women in the windows saw Rosario Montero for the last time, sitting beside her mother on the same tin-plate trunk with which she had disembarked in the town seven years before. Shaving at the window of his office, Dr. Octavio Giraldo had the impression that, in a certain way, it was a return trip to reality.

Dr. Giraldo had seen her on the afternoon of her arrival, with her shabby schoolteacher's uniform and men's shoes, ascertaining at the dock who would charge the least to carry her trunk to the school. She seemed disposed to grow old without ambition in that town whose name she had seen written for the first time—according to what she herself told—on the slip of paper that she picked from a hat when they were drawing among the eleven candidates for the six positions available. She settled down in a small room at the school with an iron bed and a washstand, spending her free time embroidering tablecloths while she boiled her mush on the little oil stove. That same year, at Christmas, she met César Montero at a school fair. He was a wild bachelor of obscure origins, grown wealthy in the lumber business, who lived in the virgin jungle among half-wild dogs and only appeared in town on rare occasions, always unshaven, with metal-tipped boots and a double-barreled shotgun. It was as if she had drawn the prize piece of paper again, Dr. Giraldo was thinking, his chin daubed with lather, when a nauseating whiff drew him out of his memories.

A flock of buzzards scattered on the opposite shore, frightened by the waves from the launch. The stench of rottenness hung over the wharf for a moment, mingling with the morning breeze, and even penetrated deep inside the houses.

"Still there, God damn it," the mayor exclaimed on the balcony of his bedroom, watching the buzzards scatter. "Fucking cow."

He covered his nose with a handkerchief, went into the room, and closed the balcony door. The smell persisted inside. Without taking off his hat, he hung the mirror on a nail and began the careful attempt at shaving his still rather inflamed cheek. A moment later the impresario of the circus knocked at the door.

The mayor had him sit down, observing him in the mirror while he shaved. He was wearing a black-and-white checkered shirt, riding breeches with leggings, and carried a whip with which he gave himself systematic taps on the knee.

"I've already had the first complaints about you people," the mayor said as he finished dragging the razor over the stubble of two weeks of desperation. "Just last night."

"What might that be?"

"That you're sending out boys to steal cats."

"That's not true," the impresario said. "Every cat that's brought to us we buy by the pound, without asking where it comes from, to feed the wild animals."

"Are they thrown in alive?"

"Oh, no," the impresario said. "That would arouse the animals' instinct of cruelty."

After washing, the mayor turned to him, rubbing his face with the towel. Until then he hadn't noticed that he was wearing rings with colored stones on almost all his fingers.

"Well, you're going to have to think up some other way," he said. "Hunt crocodiles, if you want, or take advantage of the fish that are going to waste in this weather. But live cats, don't mess with them."

The impresario shrugged his shoulders and followed the mayor to the street. Groups of men were chatting by the dock in spite of the foul odor of the cow beached in the brambles on the opposite bank.

"You sissies," the mayor shouted. "Instead of standing around there gossiping like women, you should have been busy since yesterday organizing an expedition to float that cow away."

Some men surrounded him.

"Fifty pesos," the mayor proposed, "for the one who brings me the cow's horns within an hour."

A disorder of voices exploded at the end of the dock. Some men had heard the mayor's offer and were leaping into their canoes, shouting mutual challenges as they cast off. "A hundred pesos," the mayor doubled, all enthusiastic. "Fifty for each horn." He took the impresario to the end of the dock. They both waited until the first craft reached the dunes on the other shore. Then the mayor turned to the impresario, smiling.

"This is a happy town," he said.

The impresario nodded. "The only thing wrong is something like this," the mayor went on. "People think too much about foolishness because there's nothing to do." A small group of children had slowly been forming around them.

"There's the circus," the impresario said.

The mayor was dragging him along by the arm toward the square.

"What do they do?" he asked.

"Everything," the impresario said. "We've got a complete show, for children and for adults."

"That's not enough," the mayor replied. "It's got to be within the reach of everybody."

"We've kept that in mind too," the impresario said.

Together they went to a vacant lot behind the movie theater, where they'd begun to raise the tent. Taciturn-looking men and women were taking cloths and bright colors out of the enormous trucks plated with fancy tin-work. As he followed the impresario through the crush of human beings and odds and ends, shaking everybody's hand, the mayor felt as if he were in the midst of a ship-wreck. A robust woman with resolute movements and teeth that were almost completely capped with gold examined his hand after shaking it.

"There's something strange in your future," she said.

The mayor drew his hand back, unable to repress a momentary feeling of depression. The impresario gave the woman a tap on the arm with his whip. "Leave the lieutenant alone," he said without stopping, escorting the mayor to the back of the lot, where the animals were.

"Do you believe in all that?" he asked him.

"That depends," said the mayor.

"They've never been able to convince me," the impresario said. "When a person gets mixed up in things like that he ends up believing only in human will."

The mayor contemplated the animals, who were drowsy with the heat. The cages exhaled a bitter, warm vapor and there was a kind of hopeless anguish in the measured breathing of the wild creatures. The impresario stroked the nose of a leopard with his whip as it twisted like a mime, growling.

"What's the name?" the mayor asked.

"Aristotle."

"I meant the woman," the mayor explained.

"Oh," the impresario said. "We call her Casandra, Mirror of the Future."

The mayor put on a desolate expression.

"I'd like to go to bed with her," he said.

"Everything's possible," said the impresario.

The widow Montiel opened the windows of her bedroom, murmuring: "Poor men." She put her night table in order, returned her rosary and prayer book to the drawer, and wiped the soles of her mallow-colored slippers on the jaguar skin laid out in front of the bed. Then she took a complete turn about the room to lock the dressing table, the three doors to the wardrobe, and a square cupboard on which there was a plaster Saint Raphael. Finally she locked the room.

As she was going down the broad staircase made of stones with carved labyrinths on them, she thought about the strange fate of Rosario Montero. When she saw her cross the corner of the dock with the determined composure of a schoolgirl who has been taught not to turn her head, the widow Montiel, looking out through the chinks of her balcony, sensed that something that had begun a long time ago had finally ended.

On the landing of the stairs, the country-fair bustle of her courtyard came up to meet her. To one side of the railing there was a scaffolding with cheeses wrapped in fresh leaves; farther on, in an outside gallery, sacks of salt and skins full of honey were piled up; and to the rear of the courtyard, a stable with mules and horses, and saddles on the crossbeams. The house was impregnated with a persistent beast-of-burden smell mingled with another smell, of tanning and the grinding of cane.

In the office the widow said good morning to Mr. Carmichael, who was laying out bundles of banknotes on the desk while he jotted down the amounts in the ledger. When she opened the window onto the river, the nine o'clock light entered the living room, which was overloaded with cheap decorations, great overstuffed chairs upholstered in gray, and an enlarged portrait of José Montiel, with a funeral wreath around the frame. The widow noticed the whiff of rottenness before she saw the boats on the dunes of the far shore.

"What's going on on the other bank?" she asked.

"They're trying to float a dead cow," Mr. Carmichael answered.

"So that's it," the widow said. "All night long I was dreaming about that smell." She looked at Mr. Carmichael, absorbed in his work, and added: "Now all we need is the deluge."

Mr. Carmichael spoke without raising his head.

"It started two weeks ago."

"That's right," the widow admitted. "Now we've reached the end. All that's left to do is to lie down in a grave in the sun and the dew until death comes for us."

Mr. Carmichael listened to her without interrupting his accounts. "For years we've been complaining that nothing ever happened in this town," the widow went on. "All of a sudden the tragedy starts, as if God had fixed everything so that what had stopped happening for so many years would begin to happen."

Mr. Carmichael turned to look at her from the safe and saw her with her elbows on the window, her eyes fixed on the opposite shore. She was wearing a black dress with long sleeves and was biting her nails.

"When the rain stops, things will get better," Mr. Carmichael said.

"It won't stop," the widow predicted. "Misfortunes never come alone. Didn't you see Rosario Montero?"

Mr. Carmichael had seen her. "All this is a meaningless scandal," he said. "If a person pays attention to lampoons he ends up going crazy."

"The lampoons," sighed the widow.

"They've already put mine up," Mr. Carmichael said.

"Yours?"

"Mine," Mr. Carmichael confirmed. "They put it up, quite large and quite complete, on Saturday of last week. It looked like a movie poster."

The widow pulled a chair over to the desk. "This is infamous," she exclaimed. "There's nothing that can be said about a family as exemplary as yours." Mr. Carmichael wasn't alarmed.

"Since my wife is white, the kids have come out all colors," he explained. "Just imagine, eleven of them."

"Of course," the widow said.

"Well, the lampoon said that I'm only the father of the black ones. And they listed the fathers of the others. They even involved Don Chepe Montiel, may he rest in peace."

"My husband!"

"Yours and those of four other ladies," Mr. Carmichael said.

The widow began to sob. "Luckily my daughters are far

away," she said. "They say they don't ever want to come back to this savage country where students are murdered in the street, and I tell them that they're right, that they should stay in Paris for good." Mr. Carmichael turned his chair half around, understanding that the embarrassing daily episode had begun once more.

"You've got no reason to worry," he said.

"Quite the contrary," the widow sobbed. "I'm the first one who should have packed up her goods and got away from this town, even if this land and the business that are so tied up with our misfortune are lost. No, Mr. Carmichael: I don't want gold basins to spit blood into."

Mr. Carmichael tried to console her.

"You have to face up to your responsibilities," he said. "You can't throw a fortune out the window."

"Money is the devil's dung," the widow said.

"But in this case it's also the result of Don Chepe Montiel's hard work."

The widow bit her fingers.

"You know that's not true," she replied. "It's ill-gotten wealth and the first to pay for it by dying without confession was José Montiel."

It wasn't the first time she'd said it.

"The blame, naturally, belongs to that criminal," she exclaimed, pointing to the mayor, who was going along the opposite sidewalk on the arm of the circus impresario. "But I'm the one who suffers the expiation."

Mr. Carmichael left her. He put the bundles of bills, fastened with rubber bands, into a cardboard box, and from the door to the courtyard, he called out the names of the peasants in alphabetical order.

While the men were receiving their Wednesday pay, the widow Montiel heard them pass without answering their greetings. She lived alone in the gloomy nine-room house where Big Mama had died and which José Montiel had bought without imagining that his widow would have to endure her solitude in it until death. At night, while she went about through the empty rooms with the insecticide bomb, she would find Big Mama squashing lice in the hallways, and she would ask her: "When am I going to die?" But that happy communication with the beyond only managed to increase her uncertainty, because the answers, like those of all the dead, were silly and contradictory.

A little after eleven o'clock, through her tears, the widow saw Father Ángel crossing the square. "Father, Father," she called, feeling that she was taking a final step with that call. But Father Ángel didn't hear her. He had knocked at the door of the widow Asís, on the opposite sidewalk, and the door had opened partway in a surreptitious manner to let him in.

On the porch that overflowed with the song of birds, the widow Asís was lying on a canvas chair, her face covered with a handkerchief soaked in Florida water. From the way he knocked on the door she knew it was Father Ángel, but she prolonged the momentary relief until she heard the greeting. Then she uncovered her face, devastated by insomnia.

"Forgive me, Father," she said. "I didn't expect you so early."

Father Ángel ignored the fact that he had been invited to lunch. He excused himself, a little confused, saying that he, too, had spent the morning with a headache and had preferred to cross the square before the heat began.

"It doesn't matter," the widow said. "I just meant that I didn't want you to find me looking like a wreck."

The priest took from his pocket a breviary that was losing

its binding. "If you want, you can rest a while more and I'll pray," he said. The widow objected.

"I feel better," she said.

She walked to the end of the porch, her eyes closed, and on the way back she laid out the handkerchief with extreme tidiness on the arm of the folding chair. When she sat down opposite Father Ángel she looked several years younger.

"Father," she said then, without any drama, "I have need of your help."

Father Ángel put his breviary into his pocket.

"At your service."

"It's Roberto Asís again."

Against his promise to forget about the lampoon, Roberto Asís the day before had departed until Saturday, and returned home unexpectedly that same night. Since then, until dawn, when fatigue overcame him, he had been sitting in the darkness of the room, waiting for his wife's supposed lover.

Father Ángel listened to her, perplexed.

"There's no basis for that," he said.

"You don't know the Asíses, Father," the widow replied. "They carry hell in their imaginations."

"Rebeca knows my view of the lampoons," he said. "But if you want, I can talk to Roberto Asís too."

"By no means," said the widow. "That would just be stoking the coals. On the other hand, if you could talk about the lampoons in your Sunday sermon, I'm sure that Roberto Asís would feel called upon to reflect."

Father Ángel opened his arms.

"Impossible," he exclaimed. "It would be giving the thing an importance that it doesn't have."

"Nothing's more important than avoiding a crime."

"Do you think it can reach those extremes?"

"Not only do I think so," the widow said, "but I'm sure that I won't have the means to prevent it."

A moment later they sat down at the table. A barefoot servant girl brought rice and beans, stewed vegetables, and a platter of meatballs covered with a thick brown sauce. Father Ángel served himself in silence. The hot peppers, the profound silence of the house, and the feeling of uneasiness that filled his heart at that moment carried him back to his narrow little neophyte's room in the burning noon of Macondo. On a day like that, dusty and hot, he had denied Christian burial to a hanged man whom the stiff-necked inhabitants of Macondo had refused to bury. He unbuttoned the collar of his cassock to let the sweat out.

"All right," he said to the widow. "Then make sure that Roberto Asís doesn't miss mass on Sunday."

The widow Asís promised him.

Dr. Giraldo and his wife, who never took a siesta, spent the afternoon reading a story by Dickens. They were on the inside terrace, he in a hammock, listening with his fingers interlaced behind his neck, she with the book in her lap, reading with her back to the lozenges of light where the geraniums glowed. She was reading dispassionately, with a professional emphasis, not shifting her position in the chair. She didn't raise her head until the end, but even then she remained with the book open on her knees while her husband washed in the basin of the washstand. The heat foretold a storm.

"Is it a long short story?" she asked, after thinking about it carefully.

With scrupulous movements learned in the operating room, the doctor withdrew his head from the basin. "They say it's a short novel," he said in front of the mirror, putting brilliantine on his hair. "I would say, rather, that it's a long short story." With his fingers he rubbed the vaseline into his scalp and concluded:

"Critics might say that it's a short story, but a long one."

He got dressed in white linen, helped by his wife. She could have been mistaken for an older sister, not only because of the peaceful devotion with which she attended him, but from the coldness of her eyes, which made her look like an older person. Before leaving, Dr. Giraldo showed her the list and order of his visits, should an urgent case come up, and he moved the hands on the clock chart in the waiting room: *The doctor will return at 5 o'clock.*

The street was buzzing with heat. Dr. Giraldo walked along the shady sidewalk pursued by a foreboding: in spite of the harshness of the air, it wouldn't rain that afternoon. The buzz of the harvest flies intensified the solitude of the port, but the cow had been removed and dragged off by the current, and the rotten smell had left an enormous gap in the atmosphere.

The telegrapher called to him from the hotel.

"Did you get a telegram?"

Dr. Giraldo hadn't.

" 'Advise conditions office, signed Arcofán,' " the telegrapher quoted from memory.

They went to the telegraph office together. While the physician was writing a reply, the civil servant began to nod.

"It's the muriatic acid," the doctor explained with great scientific conviction. And in spite of his foreboding, he added as consolation when he'd finished writing: "Maybe it'll rain tonight."

The telegrapher counted the words. The doctor didn't pay any attention to him. He was hanging on a fat book lying open by the key. He asked if it was a novel.

"Les Misérables, Victor Hugo," telegraphed the telegrapher. He stamped the copy of the message and came back

to the railing with the book. "I think this should last us until December."

For years Dr. Giraldo had known that the telegrapher spent his free time transmitting poems to the lady telegrapher in San Bernardo del Viento. He hadn't known that he also read her novels.

"Now, this is serious," he said, thumbing through the well-used tome which awoke in his memory the confused emotions of an adolescent. "Alexandre Dumas would have been more appropriate."

"She likes this one," the telegrapher explained.

"Have you ever met her?"

The telegrapher shook his head no.

"But it doesn't matter," he said. "I'd recognize her in any part of the world by the little jumps she always puts on the *R.*"

That afternoon Dr. Giraldo had reserved an hour for Don Sabas. He found him in bed exhausted, wrapped in a towel from the waist up.

"Was the candy good?" the doctor asked.

"It's the heat," Don Sabas lamented, turning his enormous grandmother's body toward the door. "I took my injection after lunch."

Dr. Giraldo opened his bag on a table placed by the window. The harvest flies were buzzing in the courtyard, and the house had a botanical heat. Seated in the courtyard, Don Sabas urinated like a languid spring. When the doctor put the amber liquid in the test tube, the patient felt comforted. He said, watching the analysis:

"Be very careful, Doctor. I don't want to die without finding out how this novel comes out."

Dr. Giraldo dropped a blue tablet into the sample.

"What novel?"

"The lampoons."

Don Sabas followed him with a mild look until he finished heating the tube on the alcohol lamp. He sniffed it. The faded eyes of the patient awaited him with a question.

"It's fine," the doctor said as he poured out the sample into the courtyard. Then he scrutinized Don Sabas. "Are you hung up on that business too?"

"Not me," the sick man said. "But I'm like a Jap enjoying the people's fright."

Dr. Giraldo prepared the hypodermic syringe.

"Besides," Don Sabas went on to say, "they already put mine up two days ago. The same nonsense: my sons' mess and the story about the donkeys."

The doctor tightened Don Sabas's artery with a rubber hose. The patient insisted on the story about the donkeys; he had to retell it because the doctor didn't think he'd heard it.

"It was a donkey deal I made some twenty years ago," he said. "It so happened that the donkeys I sold were found dead in the morning two days later, with no signs of violence."

He offered his arm with its flaccid flesh so that the doctor could take the blood sample. When Dr. Giraldo covered the prick with cotton, Don Sabas flexed his arm.

"Well, do you know what people made up?"

The doctor shook his head.

"The rumor went around that I had gone into the yard myself at night and shot the donkeys on the inside, sticking the revolver up their assholes."

Dr. Giraldo put the glass tube with the blood sample into his pocket.

"That story's got every appearance of being true," he said.

"It was snakes," Don Sabas said, sitting in bed like an Oriental idol. "But in any case, you have to be a fool to write a lampoon about something that everybody knows."

"That's always been a characteristic of lampoons," the doctor said. "They say what everybody knows, which is almost always sure to be the truth."

Don Sabas suffered a momentary relapse. "Really," he murmured, drying the sweat on his dizzy eyelids. He recovered immediately:

"What's happening is that there isn't a single fortune in this country that doesn't have some dead donkey behind it."

The doctor received the phrase leaning over the washstand. He saw his own reaction reflected in the water: a dental system so perfect that it didn't seem natural. Looking at the patient over his shoulder, he said:

"I've always believed, my dear Don Sabas, that shamelessness is your only virtue."

The patient grew enthusiastic. His doctor's knocks had produced a kind of sudden youth in him. "That and my sexual prowess," he said, accompanying the words with a bending of the arm that might have been a stimulant for the circulation, but which the doctor took as an express lewdness. Don Sabas gave a little bounce on his buttocks.

"That's why I die laughing at the lampoons," he went on. "They say that my sons get carried away by every little girl who begins to blossom in these woods, and I say: they're their father's sons."

Before taking his leave, Dr. Giraldo had to listen to a spectral recapitulation of Don Sabas's sexual adventures.

"Happy youth," the patient finally exclaimed. "Happy times, when a little girl of sixteen cost less than a heifer."

"Those memories will increase your sugar concentration," the doctor said.

Don Sabas opened his mouth.

"On the contrary," he replied. "They're better than your damned insulin shots."

When he reached the street the doctor had the impression that a delicious soup had begun to circulate in Don Sabas's arteries. But something else was worrying him then: the lampoons. For some days rumors had been reaching his office. That afternoon, after visiting Don Sabas, he realized that he really hadn't heard talk about anything else for a week.

He made several visits during the next hour and at every one they talked about the lampoons. He listened to the stories without making any comments, with an apparently indifferent little smile, but really trying to come to a conclusion. He was on his way back to his office when Father Ángel, who was coming from the widow Montiel's, rescued him from his reflections.

"How are those patients doing, Doctor?" Father Ángel asked.

"Mine are fine, Father," the doctor answered. "What about yours?"

Father Ángel bit his lips. He took the doctor by the arm and they began to cross the square.

"Why do you ask?"

"I don't know," the doctor said. "I've heard that there's a serious epidemic among your clientele."

Father Ángel made a deviation that to the doctor seemed deliberate.

"I've just come from the widow Montiel," he said. "That poor woman's nerves have got her worn out."

"It might be her conscience," the doctor diagnosed.

"It's an obsession with death."

Although they lived in opposite directions, Father Ángel accompanied him to his office.

"Seriously, Father"—the doctor picked up the thread—"what do you think about the lampoons?"

"I don't think about them," the priest said. "But if you

make me, I'd say that they're the work of envy in an exemplary town."

"We doctors didn't even diagnose like that in the Middle Ages," Dr. Giraldo replied.

They stopped in front of the office. Fanning himself slowly, Father Ángel asserted for the second time that day that "one mustn't give things an importance they don't have." Dr. Giraldo felt shaken by a hidden desperation.

"How do you know, Father, that there's nothing true in what the lampoons say?"

"I'd know it from the confessional."

The doctor looked him coldly in the eyes.

"All the more serious if you don't know it from the confessional," he said.

That afternoon Father Ángel noticed that in the poor people's houses, too, they were talking about the lampoons, but in a different way and even with a healthy merriment. He ate without appetite, after attending prayers with a thorn of pain in his head, which he attributed to the meatballs for lunch. Then he looked at the moral classification of the movie and, for the first time in his life, felt an obscure pride as he gave the twelve round tolls of absolute prohibition. Finally he put a stool by the street door, feeling that his head was bursting with pain, and got ready to verify publicly which ones were going into the movie contrary to his admonition.

The mayor went in. Sitting in a corner of the orchestra section, he smoked two cigarettes before the film began. His gum was completely normal, but his body still suffered from the memory of the past nights, and the wear and tear of the analgesics and cigarettes brought on nausea.

The movie house was a courtyard surrounded by a cement wall, covered with zinc plates halfway up in the orchestra, and with grass that seemed to revive every morning, fertilized with chewing gum and cigarette butts. For a moment, the mayor saw the benches of unplaned wood floating in the air over the iron grating that separated the orchestra seats from the balcony, and he noticed a vertiginous undulation in the space on the back wall that was painted white, where the film was projected.

He felt better when the lights went out. Then the strident music of the loudspeaker ceased but the vibration of the electric generator set up in a wooden shack next to the projector became more intense.

Before the movie there were some advertising slides. A trooping of muffled whispers, confused steps, and suppressed laughter moved the darkness for brief moments. Momentarily surprised, the mayor thought that that clandestine entry had the character of a subversive act against Father Ángel's rigid norms.

Although it might only have been because of the wake of cologne, he recognized the manager of the movie when he passed by.

"You bandit," he whispered, grabbing him by the arm. "You'll have to pay a special tax."

Laughing between his teeth, the manager took the next seat.

"It's a good picture," he said.

"As far as I'm concerned," the mayor said, "I'd like them all to be bad. There's nothing more boring than a moral movie."

Years before, no one had taken that censorship of the bells very seriously. But every Sunday, at the main mass, Father Ángel would point out from the pulpit and drive from the church the women who had contravened his warning during the week.

"The back door has been my salvation," the manager said.

The mayor began to follow the ancient newsreel. He spoke, pausing every time there was an item of interest on the screen.

"It's the same with everything," he said. "The priest won't give communion to women in short sleeves and they keep on wearing short sleeves, but they put on fake long sleeves before going to mass."

After the newsreel, the coming attractions for the next week were shown. They watched them in silence. At the end, the manager leaned over toward the mayor.

"Lieutenant," he whispered. "Buy this mess from me."

The mayor didn't take his eyes off the screen.

"It's not a good business."

"Not for me," the manager said. "But on the other hand, it would be a gold mine for you. It's obvious: the priest wouldn't come to you with the business of his little bells."

The mayor reflected before answering.

"It sounds good to me," he said.

But he didn't say anything concrete. He put his feet on the bench in front and lost himself in the turns of a tangled drama which in the end, according to what he thought, didn't deserve even four bells.

When he left the movie he lingered at the poolroom, where they were playing lotto. It was hot and the radio was sweating out some stony music. After drinking a bottle of soda water, the mayor went off to bed.

He walked unconcerned along the riverbank, sensing the flooded river in the darkness, the sound of its entrails and its smell of a huge animal. Opposite the bedroom door he stopped abruptly. Taking a leap backward, he unholstered his revolver.

"Come out where I can see you," he said in a tense voice, "or I'll blow your head off."

A very sweet voice came out of the darkness.

"Don't be so nervous, Lieutenant."

He stood pointing his revolver until the hidden person came out into the light. It was Casandra.

"You escaped just by a hair," the mayor said.

He had her come to the bedroom. For a long time Casandra spoke, following an irregular course. She sat on the hammock and while she spoke she took off her shoes and looked with a certain candor at her toenails, which were painted a vivid red.

Sitting opposite her, fanning himself with his cap, the mayor followed the conversation with conventional correctness. He had gone back to smoking. When it struck twelve, she lay face down in the hammock, reached out an arm adorned with a set of noisy bracelets, and pinched his nose.

"It's late, boy," she said. "Turn out the light."

The mayor smiled.

"It wasn't for that," he said.

She didn't understand.

"Do you know how to tell fortunes?" the mayor asked.

Casandra sat up in the hammock again. "Of course," she said. And then, having understood, she put her shoes on.

"But I didn't bring my cards," she said.

"Anyone who eats dirt"—the mayor smiled—"carries his own soil."

He took out a worn deck from the bottom of his suitcase. She examined each card, front and back, with serious attention. "The other cards are better," she said. "But in any case, the important thing is the message." The mayor pulled over a small table, sat down across from her, and Casandra laid out the cards.

"Love or business?" she asked.

The mayor dried the sweat on his hands.

"Business," he said.

$\mathcal{A}$ STRAY DONKEY sought shelter from the rain under the eaves of the parish house and it stayed there all night, kicking against the bedroom wall. It was a night without rest. After having managed a sudden sleep at dawn, Father Ángel woke up with the feeling that he was covered with dust. The spikenards sleeping in the drizzle, the smell of the toilet, and then the lugubrious interior of the church after the five o'clock tolling had faded away all seemed to be conspiring to make that a difficult dawn.

From the sacristy, where he dressed to say mass, he heard Trinidad harvesting her dead mice, while the stealthy weekday women entered the church. During the mass, with progressive exasperation, he noticed his acolyte's mistakes, his backwoods Latin, and he achieved at the last moment the feeling of frustration that tormented him during the evil hours of his life.

He was on his way to breakfast when Trinidad cut him off with a radiant expression. "Six more down today," she said, shaking the dead mice in the box. Father Ángel tried to rise above the confusion.

"Wonderful," he said. "At this rate we ought to find their nests and finish the extermination completely."

Trinidad had found the nests. She explained how she'd located the holes in different parts of the church, especially in the tower and the baptistery, and how she'd plugged them up with asphalt. That morning she'd found a frantic mouse beating against the wall after having looked all night for the door to its house.

They went out into the small paved courtyard, where the first shoots of spikenard were beginning to grow erect. Trinidad took her time throwing the dead mice into the toilet. When he went into his study, Father Ángel got ready to eat breakfast, having removed the small tablecloth under which every morning, like a kind of magician's trick, the breakfast that the widow Asís sent him appeared.

"I'd forgotten that I couldn't buy the arsenic," Trinidad said when she came in. "Don Lalo Moscote says that it can't be sold without a doctor's prescription."

"It won't be necessary," Father Ángel said. "They'll all smother to death in their dens."

He brought the chair over to the table and began to set up the cup, the plate with slices of plain tamales, and the coffeepot engraved with a Japanese dragon, while Trinidad was opening the window. "It's always best to be prepared in case they come back," she said. Father Ángel poured his coffee and suddenly he stopped and looked at Trinidad, with her shapeless robe and her invalid's high shoes, as she came over to the table.

"You worry too much about that," he said.

Father Ángel hadn't noticed then or earlier any indication of restlessness in the tight tangle of Trinidad's eyebrows. Unable to suppress a slight trembling of his fingers, he finished pouring himself the coffee, put in two spoonfuls of sugar, and began to stir the cup, with his gaze on the crucifix hanging on the wall.

"How long has it been since you confessed?"

"Last Friday," Trinidad answered.

"Tell me something," Father Ángel said. "Have you ever hidden any sin from me?"

Trinidad nodded no.

Father Ángel closed his eyes. Suddenly he stopped stirring the coffee, put the spoon on the plate, and grabbed Trinidad by the arm.

"Kneel down," he said.

Disconcerted, Trinidad put the cardboard box on the floor and knelt in front of him. "Say an act of contrition," Father Ángel told her, his voice having managed the paternal tone of the confessional. Trinidad clenched her fists against her breast, praying in an incomprehensible murmur until the priest laid his hand on her shoulder and said:

"All right."

"I've told a lot of lies," Trinidad said.

"What else?"

"I've had bad thoughts."

It was the order of her confession. She always enumerated the same sins in a general way and always in the same order. That time, however, Father Ángel couldn't resist the urge to dig deeper.

"For example," he said.

"I don't know." Trinidad hesitated. "Sometimes people get bad thoughts."

Father Ángel stood up.

"Did you ever get into your head the idea of taking your life?"

"Holy Mary, Mother of God," Trinidad exclaimed without raising her head, pounding on the table leg with her knuckles at the same time. Then she answered: "No, Father."

Father Ángel made her lift her head, and he noticed, with a feeling of desolation, that the girl's eyes were beginning to fill with tears.

"You mean that the arsenic is really for the mice?"

"Yes, Father."

"Then what are you crying about?"

Trinidad tried to lower her head, but he held her chin firmly. She burst into tears. Father Ángel felt them running through his fingers like warm vinegar.

"Try to calm yourself," he said. "You still haven't finished your confession."

He let her go into a silent weeping. When he felt that she had stopped crying, he said softly:

"All right, now tell me."

Trinidad blew her nose with her skirt and swallowed thick saliva that was salty with tears. When she spoke again she'd recovered her strange baritonal voice.

"My Uncle Ambrosio chases me," she said.

"How's that?"

"He wants me to let him spend a night in my bed," Trinidad said.

"Go on."

"That's all," Trinidad said. "In God's name, that's all."

"Don't swear," the priest admonished her. Then he asked with his tranquil confessor's voice, "Tell me one thing: who are you sleeping with?"

"With my mama and the others," Trinidad said. "Seven in the same room."

"What about him?"

"In the other room, with the men," Trinidad said.

"Did he ever go into your room?"

Trinidad denied it with her head.

"Tell me the truth," Father Ángel insisted. "Come on, don't be afraid: didn't he ever try to get into your bed?"

"Once."

"How did that happen?"

"I don't know," Trinidad said. "When I woke up I felt him inside under the netting, all quiet, telling me he didn't want to do anything to me, but that he wanted to sleep with me because he was afraid of the roosters."

"What roosters?"

"I don't know," Trinidad said. "That's what he told me."

"And what did you tell him?"

"That if he didn't leave I'd holler and wake everybody up."

"And what did he do?"

"Cástula woke up and asked me what was going on, and I said nothing, that I must have been dreaming, and then he stayed very quiet, like a dead man, and I almost didn't notice it when he got out from under the netting."

"He had his clothes on," the priest said in an affirmative way.

"He was the way he is when he sleeps," Trinidad said. "Only in his pants."

"He didn't try to touch you."

"No, Father."

"Tell me the truth."

"It's true, Father," Trinidad insisted. "In God's name."

Father Ángel raised her head again and looked into her moist eyes and their sad glow.

"Why did you hide it from me?"

"I was scared."

"Scared of what?"

"I don't know, Father."

He placed his hand on her shoulder and gave her some lengthy advice. Trinidad nodded approvingly. When they came to the end, he began to pray with her in a very low voice: "Our Lord Jesus Christ, true God and true Man . . ." He was praying deeply, with a certain terror, making, in the course of his prayers, a mental recounting of his life as far as memory would permit. At the moment of giving absolution, a sense of disaster had come over his spirit.

The mayor pushed open the door, shouting: "Judge." Judge Arcadio's wife appeared in the bedroom door, drying her hands on her skirt.

"He hasn't been home for two nights," she said.

"Oh, hell," the mayor said. "Yesterday he didn't show up at the office. I was looking for him everywhere on an urgent matter and no one could tell me anything about him. Don't you have any idea where he might be?"

"He must be with the whores."

The mayor left without closing the door. He went into the poolroom, where the jukebox was grinding out a sentimental song at full volume, and he went directly to the back room, shouting: "Judge." Don Roque, the owner, interrupted the operation of pouring bottles of rum into a demijohn. "He's not here, Lieutenant," he shouted. The mayor went behind the partition. Groups of men were playing cards. Nobody had seen Judge Arcadio.

"God damn it," the mayor said. "Everybody in this town knows what everybody else is doing and now that I need the judge, nobody knows where he's off to."

"Ask the one who puts up the lampoons," Don Roque said.

"Don't bug me with those pieces of paper," the mayor said.

Judge Arcadio wasn't at his office either. It was nine

o'clock, but the secretary of the court was already taking a nap on the porch. The mayor went to the police barracks, had three policemen get dressed, and sent them off to look for Judge Arcadio at the dance hall and in the rooms of the three clandestine women known to everybody. Then he went out onto the street, following no determined direction. At the barbershop, his legs spread apart in the chair and with a hot towel wrapped around his face, Judge Arcadio was sitting.

"God damn it, Judge," he shouted, "I've been looking for you for two days."

The barber removed the towel and the mayor saw a pair of bleary eyes and a chin shadowed by a three-day beard.

"You get lost while your wife is giving birth," he said.

Judge Arcadio leaped from the chair.

"Shit."

The mayor laughed noisily, pushing him back into the chair. "Don't be a fool," he said. "I've been looking for you for a different reason." Judge Arcadio stretched out again, with his eyes closed.

"Finish that up and come to the office," the mayor said. "I'll wait for you."

He sat down on a step.

"Where in hell were you?"

"Around," the judge said.

The mayor didn't patronize the barbershop. At one time he'd seen the sign nailed to the wall: *Talking Politics Prohibited,* but it had seemed natural to him. That time, however, it caught his attention.

"Guardiola," he called.

The barber cleaned the razor on his pants and remained waiting.

"What's the matter, Lieutenant?"

"Who authorized you to put that up?" the mayor asked, pointing to the notice.

"Experience," said the barber.

The mayor took a stool over to the back of the room and stood on it to remove the sign.

"Here the only one who has the right to prohibit anything is the government," he said. "We're living in a democracy."

The barber went back to his work. "No one can stop people from expressing their ideas," the mayor went on, tearing up the piece of cardboard. He threw the pieces into the wastebasket and went to the stand to wash his hands.

"So you see, Guardiola," Judge Arcadio proclaimed, "what happens to you for being such a toad."

The mayor sought out the barber in the mirror and found him absorbed in his work. He didn't lose sight of him while he dried his hands.

"The difference between before and now," he said, "is that before politicians gave the orders and now the government does."

"You heard him, Guardiola," Judge Arcadio said, his face all daubed with lather.

"Of course," the barber said.

On leaving he pushed Judge Arcadio toward the office. Under the persistent drizzle the streets seemed paved with fresh soap.

"I always thought that place was a nest of conspirators," the mayor said.

"They talk," said Judge Arcadio, "but it doesn't go beyond that."

"That's precisely what makes me suspicious," the mayor replied. "They act too tame."

"In the whole history of humanity," the judge proclaimed, "there's never been a single barber who was a conspirator. On the other hand, there hasn't been a single tailor who wasn't."

He didn't let go of Judge Arcadio's arm until he sat him in the swivel chair. The secretary came yawning into the office with a typewritten page. "That's the way," the mayor said. "Let's get to work." He pushed back his cap and took the sheet of paper.

"What's this?"

"It's for the judge," the secretary said. "It's a list of people who haven't had any lampoons put up on them."

The mayor looked at Judge Arcadio with an expression of perplexity.

"Oh, shit!" he exclaimed. "So you're hung up on that mess too."

"It's like reading detective stories," the judge apologized.

The mayor read the list.

"It's a good piece of information," the secretary explained. "The author has to be one of these. Isn't that logical?"

Judge Arcadio took the sheet away from the mayor. "This one here is such a dumb asshole," he said, addressing the mayor. Then he spoke to the secretary: "If I were putting up lampoons, the first door I'd put one on would be my own, to get rid of any suspicion about me." And he asked the mayor:

"Don't you think so, Lieutenant?"

"That's the people's mess," the mayor said. "And they're the only ones who know how it hangs together. We've got no business getting sweated up over it."

Judge Arcadio tore up the sheet, made a ball of it, and tossed it into the courtyard. "Of course."

Before the reply, the mayor had already forgotten the

incident. He put the palms of his hands on the desk and said:

"Well, the mess I want to look up in your books is this: Because of the floods, the people in the lower part of town have brought their houses to the lots located behind the cemetery, which are my property. What must I do in this case?"

Judge Arcadio smiled.

"We didn't have to come to the office for that," he said. "It's the simplest thing in the world: The town government awards the land to the settlers and pays the corresponding indemnification to the person who shows just title to it."

"I've got the documents," the mayor said.

"Then there's nothing to do but name some experts to make the appraisal," the judge said. "The town government pays."

"Who names them?"

"You can name them yourself."

The mayor walked to the door, adjusting the holster of his revolver. Watching him getting ready to leave, Judge Arcadio thought that life is nothing but a continuous succession of opportunities for survival.

"There's no reason to get nervous over such a simple matter." He smiled.

"I'm not nervous," the mayor said seriously. "But that doesn't stop it from being a mess."

"Of course, first you have to name a surrogate," the secretary put in.

The mayor turned to the judge.

"Is that true?"

"In a state of siege, it's not absolutely indispensable," the judge said. "But of course, your position would be cleaner if a surrogate handled the matter, given the coincidence that you're the owner of the lands in litigation."

"Then we'll have to appoint him," the mayor said.

Mr. Benjamín shifted his foot on the boardwalk without taking his eyes off the buzzards that were fighting over some entrails in the street. He watched the difficult movements of the creatures, ruffed and ceremonious as if they were performing an ancient dance, and he admired the representative fidelity of men who dress up as buzzards on Quinquagesima Sunday. The boy sitting at his feet daubed the other shoe with zinc oxide and rapped on the box again to order a change of feet on the boardwalk.

Mr. Benjamín, who in other days had lived by writing briefs, was never in a hurry for anything. The speed of time was imperceptible in that store where penny by penny it had been eaten up until it had been reduced to a gallon of oil and a bundle of tallow candles.

"Even though it rains it stays hot," the boy said.

Mr. Benjamín didn't agree. He wore spotless linen. The boy's back, on the other hand, was soaked in sweat.

"Heat is a mental question," Mr. Benjamín said. "The whole thing is not to pay any attention to it."

The boy made no comment. He gave another rap on the box and a moment later the job was done. Inside his gloomy store with its empty shelves, Mr. Benjamín put on his jacket. Then he put on a woven straw hat, crossed the street, protecting himself from the rain with an umbrella, and knocked at the window of the house across the way. A girl with intensely black hair and very pale skin appeared in the half-open door.

"Good morning, Mina," Mr. Benjamín said. "You still haven't had lunch?"

She said no and opened the window all the way. She was sitting in front of a large basket with pieces of wire and colored paper. In her lap she had a ball of thread, some shears, and an unfinished bouquet of artificial flowers. A record was singing on the gramophone.

"Would you do me the favor of keeping an eye on the store until I get back?" Mr. Benjamín asked.

"Will you be long?"

Mr. Benjamín was following the record.

"I'm going to the dentist's," he said. "I'll be back in half an hour."

"Oh, fine," Mina said. "The blind woman doesn't want me to hang around the window."

Mr. Benjamín stopped listening to the record. "All the songs today are the same thing," he commented. Mina picked up a finished flower at the end of a long piece of wire wrapped in green paper. She twirled it in her fingers, fascinated by the perfect correspondence between the record and the flower.

"You're a music hater," she said.

But Mr. Benjamín had left, walking on tiptoes so as not to scare off the buzzards. Mina didn't pick up her work until she saw him knock at the dentist's.

"To my way of seeing it," the dentist said, opening the door, "the chameleon has his sensibility in his eyes."

"That's possible," Mr. Benjamín admitted. "But what's that got to do with anything?"

"I just heard on the radio that blind chameleons don't change color," the dentist said.

After placing his open umbrella in a corner, Mr. Benjamín hung his jacket and hat on the same nail and got in the chair. The dentist was mixing a pink paste in his mortar.

"They say a lot of things," Mr. Benjamín said.

Not only in that instance, but under any circumstances, he spoke with a mysterious inflection.

"About chameleons?"

"About everybody."

The dentist approached the chair with the finished paste to take the impression. Mr. Benjamín took out his chipped false teeth, wrapped them in a handkerchief, and put them on the glass shelf beside the chair. Without teeth, with his narrow shoulders and skinny limbs, he had something of the saint about him. After adjusting the paste to the palate, the dentist made him close his mouth.

"That's how it is," he said, looking him in the eyes. "I'm a coward."

Mr. Benjamín tried to find some profound inspiration, but the dentist held his mouth shut. "No," he answered inside. "That's not it." He knew, like everyone, that the dentist had been the only one sentenced to death who hadn't abandoned his house. They'd perforated the walls with shots, had given him twenty-four hours to leave town, but hadn't succeeded in breaking him. He'd moved his office into an inner room and without losing his control, worked with his revolver in reach until the long months of terror passed.

While the procedure lasted, the dentist saw the same response, expressed in different degrees of anguish, appear in Mr. Benjamín's eyes. But he held his mouth shut, waiting for the paste to dry. Then he pulled off the impression.

"I wasn't referring to that," Mr. Benjamín unburdened himself. "I was referring to the lampoons."

"Oh," the dentist said. "So you're hung up on that too."

"It's a symptom of social decomposition," Mr. Benjamín said.

He'd put his false teeth back in and was starting the meticulous process of putting on his jacket.

"It's a symptom that everything's known sooner or later," the dentist said with indifference. He looked at the cloudy sky through the window and proposed: "If you want to, you can wait until it stops raining."

Mr. Benjamín hung his umbrella over his arm. "The shop's all alone," he said, observing in turn the heavy cloud loaded with drizzle. He waved goodbye with his hat.

"And get that idea out of your head, Aurelio," he said from the door. "Nobody has the right to think you're a coward because you pulled a molar for the mayor."

"In that case," the dentist said, "wait a second."

He went to the door and gave Mr. Benjamín a folded sheet of paper.

"Read it and pass it around."

Mr. Benjamín had no need to unfold the paper to know what it was about. He looked at him with his mouth open.

"Again?"

The dentist nodded his head and remained at the door until Mr. Benjamín had left.

At twelve o'clock his wife called him to lunch. Ángela, his twenty-year-old daughter, was darning socks in the dining room, which was furnished in a simple and poor way with things that seemed to have been old from their very origins. On the wooden railing that faced the courtyard there was a row of red pots with medicinal plants.

"Poor little Benjamín," the dentist said the moment he took his place at the round table. "He's hung up on the lampoons."

"Everybody is," his wife said.

"The Tovar women are leaving town," Ángela put in.

The mother collected the plates to serve the soup. "They're selling everything in a rush," she said. On breathing in the warm aroma of the soup, the dentist felt alien to his wife's worries.

"They'll be back," he said. "Shame has a short memory."

Blowing on his spoon before drinking his soup, he waited

for his daughter's comment. She was a girl of somewhat arid aspect, like him, whose look nevertheless exhaled a strange vivacity. But she didn't respond to his expectation. She talked about the circus. She said there was a man who sawed his wife in half, a midget who sang with his head in a lion's mouth, and a trapeze artist who did a triple somersault over a bank of knives. The dentist listened to her, eating in silence. At the end he promised that that night, if it didn't rain, they'd all go to the circus.

In the bedroom, while he was putting up the hammock for his siesta, he could see that the promise hadn't changed his wife's mood. She, too, was ready to leave town if they put up a lampoon about them.

The dentist listened to her without surprise. "It would be funny," he said, "if they weren't able to get rid of us with bullets, that they could get rid of us with a piece of paper stuck to the door." He took off his shoes and got into the hammock with his socks on, calming her:

"But don't you worry: there isn't the slightest danger that they'll put one up."

"They respect no one," the woman said.

"That depends," the dentist said. "They know that with me the thing has got a different price."

The woman stretched out on the bed with an air of infinite fatigue.

"If, that is, the one who's putting them up knew."

"The one who's putting them up knows," the dentist said.

The mayor was accustomed to go for days without eating. He simply forgot. His activity, feverish on occasions, was as irregular as the prolonged periods of idleness and boredom with which he wandered through the town without any aim or shut himself up in his armored office, unaware of the passage of time. Always alone, always a little adrift, he had no special interests, nor could he remember any time when he was governed by regular habits. Impelled only by an irresistible haste, he would appear at the hotel at any hour and eat whatever they served him.

That day he had lunch with Judge Arcadio. They spent the whole afternoon together until the sale of the lots was legalized. The experts did their duty. The surrogate, named on an interim basis, held his post for two hours. A little after four, as they went into the poolroom, both seemed to be coming back from a painful invasion by the future.

"So we're done with it," the mayor said, rubbing his hands.

Judge Arcadio didn't pay any attention to him. The mayor saw him feeling around on the counter and gave him an analgesic.

"A glass of water," he ordered Don Roque.

"A cold beer," Judge Arcadio corrected him, leaning his forehead on the counter.

"Or a cold beer," the mayor amended, putting the money on the counter. "You earned it working like a man."

After drinking the beer, Judge Arcadio rubbed his scalp with his fingers. The establishment was in a festive mood, waiting excitedly for the circus parade.

The mayor watched it from the poolroom, shaken by the coppers and brasses of the band. A girl with a silvery costume passed first on a midget elephant with malanga ears. Then the clowns and trapeze artists passed. It had cleared completely and the last rays of the sun were beginning to warm up the well-scrubbed afternoon. When the music stopped so the man on stilts could read the proclamation, the whole town seemed to rise up from the earth in a miraculous silence.

Father Ángel, who watched the parade from his study, kept time to the music with his head. That feeling of well-being brought back from childhood stayed with him during his meal and then into the early part of the evening, until he stopped his surveillance of entry into the movie and found himself alone in his bedroom. After praying, he remained in a grumbling ecstasy in the wicker rocking chair, not realizing when it struck nine or when the loudspeaker from the movie turned off and there remained in its stead the note of a toad. From there he went to his desk to write a summons to the mayor.

In one of the seats of honor at the circus, which he occupied at the insistence of the impresario, the mayor witnessed the opening number by the trapeze artists and an appearance of the clowns. Then Casandra appeared, dressed in black velvet and with her eyes blindfolded, offering to guess the thoughts of the public. The mayor fled. He made his routine rounds through the town and at ten o'clock went to the police barracks. There, waiting for him on notepaper in very meticulous handwriting, was the call from Father Ángel. The formality of the request alarmed him.

Father Ángel was beginning to get undressed when the mayor knocked on the door. "Golly," the curate said. "I didn't expect you so soon." The mayor took off his cap before entering.

"I like to answer my mail." He smiled.

He tossed his cap, making it spin like a disk, onto the wicker rocking chair. In earthen crocks were several bottles of soda put to cool in the water from the tub. Father Ángel took one out.

"Would you like a lemonade?"

The mayor accepted.

"I bothered you," the priest said, getting directly to the

point, "to tell you about my worries concerning your indifference to the lampoons."

He said it in such a way that it might have been interpreted as a joke, but the mayor took it literally. He wondered, perplexed, how concern over the lampoons had been able to bring Father Ángel to that point.

"It's strange, Father, that you're hung up on that too."

Father Ángel, as he searched in the drawers for a bottle-opener:

"It's not the lampoons as such that worry me," he said, a little confused, not knowing what to do with the bottle. "What worries me is—let's put it this way: a certain state of injustice that's in all this."

The mayor took the bottle from him and opened it on the buckle of his boot with a left-handed skill that drew Father Ángel's attention. He licked the overflowing foam on the neck of the bottle.

"There's a secret life," he started to say, without managing any conclusion. "Seriously, Father, I don't see what can be done."

The priest sat down at his desk. "You ought to know," he said. "After all, it's nothing new to you." He covered the room with a vague look and said in a different tone:

"It would be a matter of doing something before Sunday."

"Today's Thursday." The mayor was precise.

"I'm aware of the time," the priest replied. And he added with a hidden impulse, "But maybe it's not too late for you to fulfill your duties."

The mayor tried to twist the neck of the bottle. Father Ángel watched him go from one side of the room to the other, serious and slim, with no sign of physical aging, and he felt a definite sense of inferiority.

"As you can see," he stated, "it's not a question of anything exceptional."

It struck eleven in the belfry. The mayor waited until the last resonance had dissolved and then he leaned toward the priest, his hands resting on the desk. His face had the same repressed anxiety that his voice was to reveal.

"Look at one thing, Father," he began. "The town is calm, the people are beginning to have confidence in the authorities. Any show of force at this time would be too big a risk for something of such small importance."

Father Ángel approved with his head. He tried to explain:

"I'm referring, in a general way, to certain means of authority."

"In any case," the mayor went on without changing his stance, "I'm taking the circumstances into consideration. You know, I have six policemen here locked up in the barracks, drawing a salary without doing anything. I haven't been able to get them replaced."

"I know that," Father Ángel said. "I'm not blaming you for anything."

"Actually," the mayor went on vehemently, indifferent to interruptions, "It's no secret to anybody that three of them are common criminals, released from jail and disguised as policemen. The way things are, I'm not going to run the risk of putting them out on the streets hunting ghosts."

Father Ángel opened his arms.

"Of course, of course," he acknowledged decisively. "That, naturally, is out of the question. But why not have recourse, for example, to the good citizens?"

The mayor stretched, drinking from the bottle with listless swallows. His chest and back were soaked in sweat. He said:

"The good citizens, as you call them, are dying with laughter over the lampoons."

"Not all of them."

"Besides, it's no good alarming people over something that in the long run isn't that important. Frankly, Father," he ended good-humoredly, "until tonight it hadn't occurred to me to think that you and I would have anything to do with this mess."

Father Ángel assumed a maternal attitude. "Up to a certain point, yes," he replied, and began a laborious justification employing ripened paragraphs from the sermon he had been ordering mentally since the day before at lunch with the widow Asís.

"It's a question, if one might say so"—he came to the high point—"of a case of terrorism in the moral order."

The mayor gave an open smile. "Fine, fine," he almost interrupted him. "And it's not a case of putting philosophy onto the pieces of paper, Father." Leaving the unfinished bottle on the desk, he acceded in his most agreeable manner:

"If you put things to me this way, we'll have to see what can be done."

Father Ángel thanked him. It wasn't at all pleasant, as he revealed, to go up into the pulpit on Sunday with a worry like that. The mayor had tried to understand him. But he realized that it was getting late and he was making a night owl out of the curate.

$\mathcal{T}$HE DRUM ROLL reappeared like a specter out of the past. It burst forth in front of the poolroom at ten o'clock in the morning and held the town balancing on the very center of its gravity until the three energetic warnings were drummed at the end and anxiety was reestablished.

"Death!" exclaimed the widow Montiel, seeing doors and windows open and people pour out into the square from everywhere. "Death has come!"

Having recovered from her initial impression, she opened the balcony curtains and observed the tumult around the policeman who was preparing to read the decree. There was in the square a silence too great for the voice of the crier. In spite of the attention with which she tried to listen, the widow Montiel was only able to understand two words.

Nobody in the house could tell her what it was about.

The decree had been read with the same authoritarian ritual as always; a new order reigned in the world and she could find no one who had understood it. The cook was alarmed at her paleness.

"What was the decree about?"

"That's what I'm trying to find out, but nobody knows anything. Of course," the widow added, "ever since the world has been the world, no decree has ever brought any good."

Then the cook went out into the street and came back with the details. Starting that night and until the causes that motivated it had ceased, a curfew was reestablished. No one could go out onto the streets after eight o'clock and until five in the morning without a pass signed and stamped by the mayor. The police had orders to call Halt three times at anyone they found on the street and if they were not obeyed, they had orders to shoot. The mayor would organize patrols of civilians, appointed by him, to collaborate with the police in the nocturnal vigil.

Biting her nails, the widow Montiel asked what the reasons for the measure were.

"They didn't spell it out in the decree," the cook answered, "but everybody says it's the lampoons."

"My heart told me so," the terrified widow said. "Death is feeding on this town."

She sent for Mr. Carmichael. Obeying a force more ancient and deep-rooted than an impulse, she ordered taken from the storeroom and brought to the bedroom the leather trunk with copper rivets that José Montiel had bought for his only trip, one year before he died. Out of the closet she took some clothing, underwear, and shoes, and put everything neatly in the bottom. As she did it, she began to get the feeling of absolute repose that she had dreamed of so many times, imagining herself far away from that town and that house, in a room with a stove and a small terrace with boxes where she grew oregano, where only she had the right to remember José Montiel, and where her only worry would be to wait for Monday afternoons to read the letters from her daughters.

She had only put in clothing that was indispensable; the leather case with the scissors, the adhesive tape, and the little bottle of iodine and sewing things; and then the shoe box with her rosary and prayerbooks, and she was already tormented by the idea that she was taking more things than God could pardon her for. Then she put the plaster Saint Raphael into a stocking, arranged it carefully among her clothes, and locked the trunk.

When Mr. Carmichael arrived he found her wearing her most modest attire. That day, like a promissory sign, Mr. Carmichael wasn't carrying his umbrella. But the widow didn't notice. From her pocket she took out all the keys of the house, each with its identification typed on a piece of cardboard, and gave them to him, saying:

"Into your hands I place the sinful world of José Montiel. Do with it whatever you feel like doing."

Mr. Carmichael had feared that moment for a long time.

"You mean," he struggled to say, "that you want to go off somewhere while all these things are happening."

The widow answered him with a calm voice, but quite decisively:

"I'm going away forever."

Mr. Carmichael, without showing his alarm, gave her a synthesis of the situation. José Montiel's estate had not been settled. Many of the possessions acquired in any old way and without time to observe formalities had an uncertain legal status. Until order could be put into that chaotic fortune, of which José Montiel himself didn't even have the vaguest notion in his last years, it would be impossible to settle the inheritance. The oldest son, in his consular post in Germany, and her two daughers, fascinated by the delirious fleshpots of Paris, would have to return or give someone power of attorney in order to evaluate their rights. Until then nothing could be sold.

The momentary illumination of the labyrinth where she had been lost for two years didn't move the widow Montiel that time.

"It doesn't matter," she insisted. "My children are happy in Europe and want nothing to do with this country of savages, as they call it. If you want, Mr. Carmichael, make a single bundle out of everything you find in this house and throw it to the hogs."

Mr. Carmichael didn't contradict her. With the pretense that, in any case, certain things had to be prepared for the trip, he went for the doctor.

"Now we'll see what your patriotism is made of, Guardiola."

The barber and the group of men chatting in the barbershop recognized the mayor before they saw him at the door. "And you people too," he went on, pointing to the two youngest. "Tonight you'll have the rifles you've wanted so much; let's see if you're rotten enough to turn them against us." It was impossible to mistake the cordial tone of his words.

"A broom would be better," the barber answered. "For hunting witches there's no better rifle than a broom."

He didn't even look at him. He was shaving the neck of the first customer of the morning, and he wasn't taking the mayor seriously. Only when he saw him checking on who in the group were reservists and could therefore handle a rifle did the barber understand that, indeed, he was one of the chosen.

"Is it true, Lieutenant, that you're going to involve us in this mess?" he asked.

"Oh, shit," the mayor answered. "You spend your lives whispering for a rifle and now that you've got one, you can't believe it."

He stopped in front of the barber, from where he could dominate the whole group in the mirror. "Seriously," he said, shifting to an authoritarian tone. "This afternoon at six, first-class reservists will report to the barracks." The barber faced him through the mirror.

"What if I come down with pneumonia?" he asked.

"We'll cure you in jail," the mayor answered.

The phonograph in the poolroom was twisting out a sentimental bolero. The place was empty, but on some tables there were bottles and half-finished glasses.

"Now, for sure," Don Roque said, seeing the mayor enter, "it really is a mess. We'll have to close at seven."

The mayor went straight to the back of the room, where the card tables were also deserted. He opened the door to the toilet, looked into the storeroom, and then came back to the bar. Passing by the pool table, he unexpectedly lifted the cloth that covered it, saying:

"All right, stop being jackasses."

Two boys came out from under the table, shaking the dust off their pants. One of them was pale. The other, younger, had his ears all red. The mayor pushed them gently toward the tables at the entrance.

"So you already know," he told them. "Six o'clock at the barracks."

Don Roque stayed behind the counter.

"With this mess," he said, "a person will have to turn to smuggling."

"It's just for two or three days," the mayor said.

The manager of the movie theater caught up to him on

the corner. "This is all I needed," he shouted. "After twelve bells, one bugle." The mayor patted him on the shoulder and tried to continue on.

"I'm going to expropriate you," he said.

"You can't," the manager said. "The movies aren't a public service."

"In a state of siege," the mayor said, "even the movies can be declared a public service."

Only then did he stop smiling. He ran up the barracks stairs two steps at a time and when he got to the second floor he opened his arms and laughed again.

"Shit!" he exclaimed. "You too?"

Collapsed in a folding chair, with the insouciance of an Oriental monarch, was the circus impresario. He was ecstatically smoking a sea dog's pipe. As if it were he who was in his own home, he signaled the mayor to sit down.

"Let's talk business, Lieutenant."

The mayor pulled over a chair and sat down opposite him. Holding the pipe in the hand paved with colored stones, the impresario made an enigmatic sign to him.

"Can we speak with absolute frankness?"

The mayor nodded that he could.

"I knew it yesterday when I saw you shaving," the impresario said. "Well—I'm accustomed to knowing people, and I know that this curfew, for you . . ."

The mayor was examining him with a definite aim at amusement.

"For me, on the other hand, having paid for the installation and having to feed seventeen people and nine animals, it's simply a disaster."

"So?"

"I propose," the impresario replied, "that you set the curfew for eleven o'clock and we'll split the profits from the evening performance."

The mayor kept on smiling, without changing his position in the chair.

"I suppose," he said, "that it wasn't hard for you to find someone in town who said I'm a thief."

"It's a legitimate business deal," the impresario protested.

He didn't notice at what moment the mayor took on a serious expression.

"We'll talk about it Monday," the lieutenant said in an imprecise way.

"By Monday I'll have hocked my very hide," the impresario replied. "We're oh so poor."

The mayor took him to the stairs, patting him softly on the shoulder. "You don't have to tell me," he said. "I know all about the business." Once by the stairs, he said in a consoling tone:

"Send Casandra to me tonight."

The impresario tried to turn around, but the hand on his shoulder exercised a decided pressure.

"Of course," he said. "That's deducted."

"Send her," the mayor insisted, "and we'll talk tomorrow."

Mr. Benjamín pushed the screen door with the tips of his fingers, but he didn't go into the house. He exclaimed with a secret exasperation:

"The windows, Nora."

Nora Jacob—mature and large—with her hair cut like a man's, was lying in front of the electric fan in the half-dark living room. She was waiting for Mr. Benjamín for lunch. On hearing the call, she got up laboriously and opened the four windows to the street. A gush of heat entered the room, tiled with the same angular peacock indefinitely repeated, and its furniture covered with flowered cloth. Every detail bespoke a poor luxury.

"What's true," she asked, "in what people are saying?"

"They're saying so many things."

"About the widow Montiel." Nora Jacob was more precise. "They're going around saying that she's gone crazy."

"I think she's been crazy for some time now," Mr. Benjamín said. And he added with a certain disillusion, "That's how it is: this morning she tried to jump off her balcony."

The table, completely visible from the street, was set with a place at either end. "God's punishment," said Nora Jacob, clapping her hands for lunch to be served. She brought the fan into the dining room.

"The house has been full of people ever since this morning," Mr. Benjamín said.

"It's a good chance to see the inside," replied Nora Jacob.

A black girl, her head full of red bows, brought the steaming soup to the table. The smell of chicken invaded the dining room and the temperature became intolerable. Mr. Benjamín tucked his napkin into his collar, saying: "Your health." He tried to drink from the scalding spoon.

"Blow on it, don't be a fool," she said impatiently. "Besides, you've got to take your jacket off. Your scruples about not coming into the house with the windows closed is going to make us die of the heat."

"It's more indispensable than ever now," he said. "No one will be able to say that he hasn't seen from the street every move I make when I'm in your house."

She opened up her splendid orthopedic smile, with sealing-wax gums. "Don't be ridiculous," she exclaimed. "As far as I'm concerned, they can say whatever they want." When she was able to drink the soup, she went on talking during the pauses.

"I might be worried, true, about what they'd say about

Mónica," she concluded, referring to her fifteen-year-old daughter, who hadn't been home for vacation ever since she'd gone away to school for the first time. "But they can't say anything about me that everybody doesn't already know."

Mr. Benjamín didn't give her his usual look of disapproval. They drank their soup in silence, separated by the six feet of the table, the shortest distance he would ever permit, especially in public. When she had been away at school, twenty years before, he would write her long and conventional letters, which she answered with passionate notes. During a vacation, at a picnic, Néstor Jacob, completely drunk, had dragged her into a corner of the corral by the hair and declared to her without alternatives: "If you don't marry me I'll shoot you." They got married at the end of her vacation. Ten years later they'd separated.

"In any case," Mr. Benjamín said, "there's no reason to stimulate people's imaginations with closed doors."

He stood up when he'd finished his coffee. "I'm going," he said. "Mina must be desperate." From the door, putting on his hat, he exclaimed:

"This house is burning up."

"That's what I've been telling you," she said.

She waited until from the last window she saw him take his leave with a kind of blessing. Then she brought the fan into the bedroom, closed the door, and got completely undressed. Finally, as on every day after lunch, she went into the adjoining bathroom and sat on the toilet, alone with her secret.

Four times a day she saw Néstor Jacob pass by the house. Everybody knew that he was living with another woman, that he had four children by her, and that he was considered an exemplary father. Several times over the past few years, he had passed by the house with the children, but never with the woman. She'd seen him grow thin, old, and pale, and turn into a stranger whose intimacy of past times seemed inconceivable. Sometimes, during her solitary siestas, she'd desired him again in a pressing way: not as she saw him pass by the house, but as he'd been during the time that preceded Mónica's birth, when his brief and conventional love had still not made him intolerable to her.

Judge Arcadio slept until noon. So he didn't hear about the decree until he got to his office. His secretary, on the other hand, had been alarmed since eight o'clock, when the mayor asked him to draw up the document.

"No matter what," Judge Arcadio reflected after finding out the details, "it's been drawn up in drastic terms. It wasn't necessary."

"It's the same decree as always."

"That's true," the judge admitted. "But things have changed, and terms have changed too. The people must be frightened."

Nevertheless, as he discovered later on while playing cards at the poolroom, fear wasn't the predominant feeling. It was, rather, a feeling of collective victory in the confirmation that was in everyone's consciousness: things hadn't changed. Judge Arcadio couldn't draw out the mayor when he left the poolroom.

"So the lampoons weren't worth the trouble," he told him. "The people are happy."

The mayor took him by the arm. "Nothing's being done against the people," he said. "It's a routine matter." Judge Arcadio was in despair over those ambulatory conversations. The mayor marched along with a resolute step, as if he were on urgent business, and then after much walking you realized that he wasn't going anywhere.

"This won't last for a whole lifetime," he went on. "By

Sunday we'll have the clown who's behind the lampoons locked up. I don't know why, but I keep thinking that it's a woman."

Judge Arcadio didn't think so. In spite of the negligence with which his secretary had gathered information, he'd come to an overall conclusion: the lampoons weren't the work of a single person. They didn't seem to follow any set pattern. Some, in the last few days, presented a new twist: they were drawings.

"It might not be a man or a woman," Judge Arcadio concluded. "It might be different men and different women, all acting on their own."

"Don't complicate things for me, Judge," the mayor said. "You ought to know that in every mess, even if a lot of people are involved, there's always one who's to blame."

"Aristotle said that, Lieutenant," Judge Arcadio replied. And added with conviction, "In any case, the measures seem extreme to me. The ones who are putting them up will simply wait for the curfew to be over."

"That doesn't matter," the mayor said. "In the end we have to preserve the principle of authority."

The recruits had begun to gather at the barracks. The small courtyard with its high concrete walls spattered with dry blood and bullet holes recalled the times when there weren't enough cells and prisoners were kept outdoors. That afternoon the unarmed policemen were wandering through the halls in their shorts.

"Rovira," the mayor shouted from the door. "Bring those boys something to drink."

The policeman began to get dressed.

"Rum?" he asked.

"Don't be a fool," the mayor shouted on his way to the armored office. "Ice water."

The recruits were smoking, sitting around the courtyard.

Judge Arcadio observed them from the railing on the second floor.

"Are they volunteers?"

"Fat chance," the mayor said. "I had to drag them out from under their beds, as if they were being drafted."

"Well, they seem to have been recruited by the opposition," he said.

The heavy steel doors of the office exhaled an icy breath on being opened. "That means they're good for a fight," the mayor said, smiling, after he turned on the lights in his private fortress. At one end there was an army cot, a glass pitcher and a tumbler on a chair, and a chamber pot under the cot. Leaning against the bare concrete walls were rifles and submachine guns. The room had no ventilation except for the narrow, high peepholes from which one could dominate the docks and the two main streets. At the other end was the desk, beside the safe.

The mayor worked the combination.

"And that's nothing," he said. "I'm going to give them all rifles."

The policeman came in behind them. The mayor gave him a few bills, saying, "Bring each one two packs of cigarettes too." When they were alone once more, he addressed Judge Arcadio again.

"What do you think of the mess?"

The judge answered pensively:

"A useless risk."

"People will stand with their mouths open," the mayor said. "I think, besides, that these poor fellows won't know what to do with the rifles."

"They may be confused," the judge admitted, "but that won't last long."

He made an effort to repress the feeling of emptiness in his stomach. "Be careful, Lieutenant," he reflected. "Don't be the one to ruin everything." The mayor took him out of the office with an enigmatic gesture.

"Don't be a damned fool, Judge," he whispered in his ear. "They'll only have blank cartridges."

When they went down to the courtyard the lights were on. The recruits were drinking sodas under the dirty light bulbs, against which the horse flies hurled themselves. Strolling from one end to the other of the courtyard, where there were still a few puddles of stagnant water, the mayor explained to them in a paternal tone what their mission for that evening consisted of: They would be stationed in pairs on the main corners with orders to fire on anyone, man or woman, who disobeyed the three commands to halt. He recommended valor and prudence. After midnight they would be brought food. The mayor hoped that with God's help, everything would come off without any trouble and that the town would know how to appreciate that effort of the authorities in the interests of social order.

Father Ángel was getting up from the table when eight o'clock struck in the belfry. He turned out the courtyard light, threw the bolt, and made the sign of the cross over his breviary: "In the name of God." In a distant courtyard a curlew sang. Dozing in the cool of the porch beside the cages covered with dark cloths, the widow Asís heard the second toll and without opening her eyes asked: "Did Roberto come in yet?" A maid squatting against the door-frame answered that he'd been in bed since seven o'clock. A little while before, Nora Jacob had turned down the volume on the radio and was in ecstasy over some tenuous music that seemed to be coming from a clean and comfortable place. A voice too distant to seem real shouted a name on the horizon and the dogs began to bark.

The dentist hadn't finished listening to the news.

Remembering that Ángela was doing a crossword puzzle under the bulb in the courtyard, without looking he ordered her: "Close the main door and go finish that in your room." His wife awoke, startled.

Roberto Asís, who in fact had gone to bed at seven o'clock, got up to look at the square through the half-open window, and he only saw the dark almond trees and the last light that was going out on the widow Montiel's balcony. His wife turned on the night light and with a muffled whisper made him go back to bed. A solitary dog continued barking until after the fifth toll.

In the hot bedroom piled high with empty cans and dusty bottles, Don Lalo Moscote was snoring with the newspaper spread out over his belly and his glasses on his forehead. His paralytic wife, shaken by the memory of other nights like that, shooed mosquitoes with a rag while she mentally counted the hour. After the distant shouts, the barking of the dogs, and the stealthy running, silence took over.

"Make sure there's Coramine," Dr. Giraldo instructed his wife, who was putting emergency drugs into his bag before going to bed. They were both thinking about the widow Montiel, rigid as a corpse under the last load of Luminal. Only Don Sabas, after a long conversation with Mr. Carmichael, had lost his sense of time. He was still in his office, weighing the next day's breakfast on the scale, when the seventh bell tolled and his wife came out of the bedroom with her hair in disarray. The river stopped. "On a night like this," someone murmured in the dark at the instant the eighth bell tolled, deep, irrevocable, and something that had begun to sputter fifteen minutes before went out completely.

Dr. Giraldo closed the book until the curfew bugle stopped vibrating. His wife put the bag on the night table, lay down with her face to the wall, and put out her lamp.

The doctor opened the book but he didn't read. Both were breathing fitfully, alone in a town that the measureless silence had reduced to the dimensions of a bedroom.

"What are you thinking about?"

"Nothing," the doctor replied.

He didn't concentrate any more until eleven o'clock, when he went back to the same page where he'd been when eight began to strike. He turned down the corner of the page and put the book on the table. His wife was sleeping. In other times they had both stayed up till dawn, trying to figure out the place and circumstances of the shooting. Several times the sound of boots and weapons reached the door of their house and they both waited, sitting in bed, for the spray of lead that would knock down the door. Many nights, after they had learned how to distinguish among the infinite varieties of the terror, they had stayed awake with their heads on a pillow stuffed with clandestine fliers to be distributed. One dawn they heard the same stealthy preparations that precede a serenade, and then the mayor's weary voice: "Not there. He's not mixed up in anything." Dr. Giraldo turned out the lamp and tried to sleep.

The drizzle started after midnight. The barber and another recruit, stationed on the corner by the docks, abandoned their post and sought shelter under the eaves of Mr. Benjamín's store. The barber lighted a cigarette and examined the rifle in the light of the match. It was a new weapon.

"It's a madeinusa," he said.

His companion lighted several matches in search of the brand on his carbine, but he couldn't find it. A gutter by the eaves burst onto the butt of the weapon and produced a hollow impact. "What a strange mess," he murmured, drying it with his sleeve. "The two of us here, each with a rifle, getting wet." In the extinguished town no sounds could be perceived other than that of the water from the eaves.

"There are nine of us," the barber said. "Seven of them, counting the mayor, but three of them locked up in the barracks."

"A while back I was thinking the same thing," the other one said.

The mayor's flashlight made them brutally visible, crouched against the wall, trying to protect their weapons from the drops that were bursting on their shoes like bird shot. They recognized him when he put out the light and came in under the eaves. He was wearing a trench coat and had a submachine gun slung over his shoulder. A policeman was with him. After looking at his watch, which he wore on his right wrist, he ordered the policeman:

"Go to the barracks and see what's happened to the food."

With the same energy that he would have given a battle command, the policeman disappeared in the rain. Then the mayor sat down on the ground beside the recruits.

"Any messes?" he asked.

"Nothing," answered the barber.

The other man offered the mayor a cigarette before lighting his. The mayor turned it down.

"How long are you going to keep us at this, Lieutenant?"

"I don't know," the mayor said. "For now, until curfew is over. We'll see what happens tomorrow."

"Until five o'clock!" the barber exclaimed.

"Oh, no," the other one said. "Me, who's been on his feet since four in the morning."

A dogfight reached them through the murmur of the rain. The mayor waited until the tumult was over and there was only one solitary bark. He turned to the recruit with a depressed air.

"Don't tell me; I've spent half my life in this mess," he said. "I'm collapsing from lack of sleep."

"For no reason," the barber said. "This hasn't got any head or tail to it. It's like something women do."

"I'm beginning to think the same thing," the mayor sighed.

The policeman returned to inform them that they were waiting for the rain to stop to give out the food. Then he delivered another message: a woman, caught without a pass, was waiting for the mayor at the barracks.

It was Casandra. She was sleeping in the folding chair, wrapped in a rubber cape in the small room lighted by the mournful bulb on the balcony. The mayor tweaked her nose. She gave a moan, shuddered in a start of desperation, and opened her eyes.

"I was dreaming," she said.

The mayor turned on the light in the room. Protecting her eyes with her hands, the woman twisted, grumbling, and for an instant he suffered her silver-colored nails and shaved armpits.

"You're a fine one," she said. "I've been here since eleven o'clock."

"I expected to see you at the room," the mayor apologized.

"I didn't have a pass."

Her hair, copper-colored two nights before, was silver gray now. "I forgot completely." The mayor smiled, and after hanging up his raincoat, he took a seat beside her. "I hope they haven't thought that you're the one who's putting up the papers." The woman had recovered her relaxed manner.

"I wish they had," she replied. "I adore strong emotions."

Suddenly the mayor seemed lost in the room. With a defenseless air, cracking his knuckles, he murmured: "You have to do me a favor." She scrutinized him.

"Just between the two of us," the mayor went on, "I want you to deal the cards to see if it's possible to find out who's responsible for this mess."

She turned her head away. "I understand," she said after a brief silence. The mayor urged her:

"I'm doing it for you people more than anything."

She nodded.

"I've already done it."

The mayor couldn't hide his anxiety. "It's something very strange," Casandra went on with calculated melodrama. "The signs were so obvious that I was frightened after having them on the table." Even her breathing had become affected.

"Who is it?"

"It's the whole town and it's nobody."

HE SONS of the widow Asís came to mass on Sunday. They were seven in addition to Roberto Asís. All founded in the same mold: heavy and rough, with something mulish in their will for hard work, and docile to their mother with a blind obedience. Roberto Asís, the youngest and the only son who had married, had only a lump on the bone of his nose in common with his brothers. With his delicate health and his conventional ways, he was a kind of consolation prize for the daughter that the widow Asís had grown tired of waiting for.

In the kitchen, where the seven Asíses had unloaded the animals, the widow walked among an outpouring of trussed-up chickens, vegetables and cheeses and brown sugar loaves and strips of salted meat, giving instructions to the servant girls. Once the kitchen was cleared, she ordered them to pick out the best of everything for Father Ángel.

The curate was shaving. From time to time he reached his hand out into the courtyard so he could wet his chin with the drizzle. He was getting ready to finish when two barefoot girls pushed open the door without knocking and in front of him poured out several ripe pineapples, red plantains, sugar loaves, cheese, and a basket of vegetables and fresh eggs.

Father Ángel winked at them. "This," he said, "looks like Br'er Rabbit's dream." The younger of the girls, with her eyes all wide, pointed at him:

"Priests shave too!"

The other one led her to the door. "What did you think?" The curate smiled, and added seriously: "We're human too." Then he contemplated the provisions scattered on the floor and understood that only the house of Asís was capable of such prodigality.

"Tell the boys," he almost shouted, "that God will give it back to them in health."

Father Ángel, who after forty years in the priesthood had not learned to dominate the nervousness that precedes solemn acts, put away the instruments without finishing shaving. Then he picked up the provisions and piled them under the jar rack and went into the sacristy, drying his hands on his cassock.

The church was full. In the two pews closest to the pulpit, donated by them and with their respective names engraved on copper plates, were the Asíses, with mother and sister-in-law. When they reached the church, together for the first time in several months, one would have thought they were coming on horseback. Cristóbal Asís, the eldest, who had arrived from the ranch a half hour before and hadn't had time to shave, was still wearing his riding boots and spurs. Seeing that forest giant, the public but never confirmed story that César Montero was the secret son of old Adalberto Asís seemed true.

In the sacristy Father Ángel suffered a contretemps: the liturgical ornaments weren't in their place. The acolyte found him upset, going through drawers while he carried on an obscure argument with himself.

"Call Trinidad," the priest ordered him, "and ask her where she put the stole."

He was forgetting that Trinidad had been ill since Saturday. Most certainly, the acolyte thought, she'd taken some things home to fix. Father Ángel then put on the ornaments reserved for funerals. He couldn't manage to concentrate. When he went up into the pulpit, impatient and still breathing irregularly, he could see that the arguments that had ripened in the days preceding wouldn't have as much strength of conviction now as in the solitude of his room.

He spoke for ten minutes. Stumbling over his words, surprised by a flock of ideas that didn't fit into the previous patterns, he spotted the widow Asís, surrounded by her sons. It was as if he had recognized them several centuries later in some hazy family photograph. Only Rebeca Asís, calming her splendid bust with the sandalwood fan, seemed human and contemporary to him. Father Ángel finished his sermon without referring directly to the lampoons.

The widow Asís remained rigid for a few short minutes, taking her wedding ring off and putting it back on with a secret exasperation, while the mass picked up again. Then she crossed herself, stood up, and left the church by the central nave, followed tumultuously by her sons.

On a morning like that, Dr. Giraldo could understand the inner mechanism of suicide. It was drizzling noiselessly, the troupial was whistling in the house next door, and his wife was talking while he brushed his teeth.

"Sundays are strange," she said, setting the table for

breakfast. "It's as if they were hung up quartered: they smell of raw animals."

The doctor put his razor together and began to shave. His eyes were moist and his eyelids puffy. "You're not sleeping well," his wife told him. And she added with a soft bitterness: "One of these Sundays you're going to wake up an old man." She'd put on a frayed robe and her head was covered with curlers.

"Do me a favor," he said. "Shut up."

She went to the kitchen, put the coffeepot on the stove, and waited for it to boil, hanging first on the whistle of the troupial and a moment later on the sound of the shower. Then she went to the bedroom so her husband would find his clothes ready when he came out of the bathroom. When she brought the breakfast to the table, she saw that he was ready to leave, and he looked a little younger with his khaki pants and sport shirt.

They ate breakfast in silence. Toward the end he examined her with affectionate attention. She was drinking her coffee with her head down, a little trembly with resentment.

"It's my liver," he excused himself.

"Nothing justifies snapping," she replied without raising her head.

"I must be drunk," he said. "The liver gets all clogged up with this rain."

"You always say the same thing," she made clear, "but you never do anything. If you don't open your eyes," she added, "you'll have to heal thyself."

He seemed to believe her. "In December," he said, "we'll be two weeks at sea." He observed the drizzle through the openings of the wooden grating that separated the dining room from the courtyard, saddened by the persistence of October, and added: "Then, at least for four months, there won't be any Sundays like this one." She piled up the plates before taking them into the kitchen. When she came back to the dining room she found him with his straw hat on, getting his bag ready.

"So the widow Asís came out of church again," he said.

His wife had told him before he started brushing his teeth, but he hadn't paid any attention.

"They've gone about three times this year," she confirmed. "Evidently they haven't found any better way to entertain themselves."

The doctor bared his rigorous dental system.

"Rich people are crazy."

Some women, on the way home from church, had gone in to visit the widow Montiel. The doctor greeted the group that remained in the living room. A murmur of laughs followed him to the landing. Before knocking on the door, he realized that there were other women in the bedroom. Someone told him to come in.

The widow Montiel was sitting up, her hair loose, holding the edge of the sheet against her breast. She had a mirror and a comb in her lap.

"So you decided to come to the party too," she said to the physician.

"She's celebrating her fifteenth birthday," said one of the women.

"Eighteenth," the widow Montiel corrected with a sad smile. Lying down in bed again, she covered herself up to the neck. "Of course," she added good-humoredly, "no men have been invited. Much less you, Doctor; it's bad luck."

The doctor laid his wet hat on the dresser. "You did well," he said, observing the patient with a pensive pleasure. "I've just realized that I've got nothing to do here." Then, turning to the group, he excused himself:

"Will you allow me?"

When she was alone with him, the widow Montiel took on the bitter expression of a sick woman again. But the doctor didn't seem to notice. He continued speaking in the same festive tone while he laid out on the night table the things he was taking from his bag.

"Please, Doctor," the widow begged, "no more injections. I'm like a sieve."

"Injections"—the doctor smiled—"are the best thing ever invented for the feeding of doctors."

She smiled too.

"Believe me," she said, touching her buttocks through the sheet, "this whole part of me is raw. I can't even touch it."

"Don't touch it," the doctor said.

Then she smiled openly.

"Talk seriously, even if only on Sundays, Doctor."

The physician uncovered her arm to take her blood pressure.

"My doctor won't let me," he said. "It's bad for the liver."

While he was taking her pressure, the widow observed the dial on the sphygmomanometer with a childish curiosity. "That's the funniest watch I've ever seen," she said. The doctor remained intent on the needle until he finished squeezing the ball.

"It's the only one that tells exactly what time to get up," he said.

When he'd finished and was rolling up the tubes of the sphygmomanometer, he observed the face of the patient minutely. He put a bottle of white pills on the table with the indication that she take one every twelve hours. "If you don't want any more injections," he said, "there won't be any more injections. You're in better health than I am." The widow made a gesture of impatience.

"I never had anything," she said.

"I believe you," the physician replied, "but we've had to invent something in order to justify the bill."

Ignoring the comment, the widow asked:

"Do I have to stay in bed?"

"On the contrary," the doctor said, "I absolutely forbid it. Go down to the living room and take care of your visitors as you should. Besides," he added with a mischievous voice, "there are a lot of things to talk about."

"Good heavens, Doctor," she exclaimed, "don't be so gossipy. You must be the one who's putting up the lampoons."

Dr. Giraldo reveled in the idea. On leaving, he cast a furtive look at the leather trunk with copper rivets in the corner of the bedroom, ready for the trip. "And bring me something back," he shouted from the door, "when you return from your trip around the world." The widow had taken up the patient labor of untangling her hair again.

"Of course, Doctor."

She didn't go down to the living room. She stayed in bed until the last visitor had left. Then she got dressed. Mr. Carmichael found her eating by the half-opened balcony door.

She replied to his greeting without taking her eyes off the balcony. "Deep down," she said, "I like that woman: she's valiant." Mr. Carmichael also looked toward the house of the widow Asís, where the doors and windows hadn't been opened at eleven o'clock.

"It has something to do with her nature," he said. "With insides like hers, made for males only, she couldn't be any other way." Turning his attention to the widow Montiel, he added: "And you're like a rose too."

She seemed to confirm it with the freshness of her smile. "Do you know something?" she asked. And in the face of

Mr. Carmichael's indecision she got ahead of the answer:

"Dr. Giraldo is convinced that I'm crazy."

"You don't say!"

The widow nodded yes. "It wouldn't surprise me," she went on, "if he'd already talked to you about some way to send me to the insane asylum." Mr. Carmichael didn't know how to untangle himself from the confusion.

"I haven't been out of the house all morning," he said.

He dropped into the soft leather easy chair placed beside the bed. The widow remembered José Montiel in that chair, struck down by a cerebral congestion fifteen minutes before dying. "In that case," she said, shaking off the bad memory, "you might call him this afternoon." And she changed the subject with a lucid smile:

"Did you talk to my good friend Sabas?"

Mr. Carmichael nodded yes.

In fact, on Friday and Saturday he had taken soundings in the abyss that was Don Sabas, trying to find out what his reaction would be if José Montiel's estate were put up for sale. Don Sabas—Mr. Carmichael supposed—seemed ready to buy it. The widow listened without showing any signs of impatience. If it wasn't next Wednesday, it would be Wednesday of the following week, she admitted with a relaxed firmness. In any event, she was ready to leave town before October was over.

The mayor unholstered his revolver with an instantaneous movement of his left hand. Right down to the last muscle his body was ready to fire, when he awoke completely and recognized Judge Arcadio.

"Shit!"

Judge Arcadio was petrified.

"Don't you ever mess up like that again," the mayor said, putting the revolver away. He fell back into the canvas chair. "My hearing works better when I'm asleep."

"The door was open," Judge Arcadio said.

The mayor had forgotten to close it at dawn. He was so tired that he'd dropped into the chair and fallen asleep instantly.

"What time is it?"

"It's going on twelve," Judge Arcadio said.

There was still a tremulous chord in his voice.

"I'm dying for sleep," the mayor said.

Twisting in a long yawn, he had the impression that time had stopped. In spite of his diligence, of his sleepless nights, the lampoons continued. That dawn he'd found a piece of paper stuck to the door of his room: *Don't waste gunpowder on buzzards, Lieutenant.* On the street they were saying aloud that the very ones who made up the patrols were posting the lampoons to break the boredom of their rounds. The town—the mayor had thought—is dying with laughter.

"Shake it off," Judge Arcadio said, "and let's go get something to eat."

But he wasn't hungry. He wanted to sleep another hour and take a bath before going out. Judge Arcadio, on the other hand, fresh and clean, was going back home to have lunch. When he passed by the room, since the door was open, he'd gone in to ask the mayor for a pass to be on the streets after the curfew.

The lieutenant said simply: "No." Then, in a paternal way, he justified himself:

"It's better for you to be safe at home."

Judge Arcadio lighted a cigarette. He stood contemplating the flame of the match, waiting for the rancor to decline, but he found nothing to say.

"Don't take it so badly," the mayor added. "Believe me, I'd like to change places with you, going to bed at eight o'clock at night and getting up whenever I felt like it."

"Of course," said the judge. And he added with accentuated irony: "That's all I needed: a new daddy at the age of thirty-five."

"Judge." Judge Arcadio turned toward him and they looked into each other's eyes. "I'm not going to give you the pass. Understand?"

The judge bit his cigarette and began to say something, but he repressed the impulse. The mayor heard him going slowly down the stairs. Suddenly, leaning over, he shouted:

"Judge!"

There was no answer.

"We're still friends," the mayor shouted.

He didn't get any answer that time either.

He remained leaning over, waiting for the reaction of Judge Arcadio, until the door closed and he was alone with his memories once more. He made no effort to sleep. He was sleepless in the middle of the day, bogged down in a town that remained impenetrable and alien, many years after he had taken charge of its fate. On the dawn when he had disembarked furtively with an old cardboard suitcase tied with cord and the order to make the town submit at all costs, it was he who'd come to know terror. His only pretext was a letter for an obscure partisan of the government, whom he was to meet the following day sitting in his shorts by the door of a rice bin. With his instructions and the implacable will of the three hired assassins who accompanied him, the task had been accomplished. That afternoon, though, unaware of the invisible cobweb that time had been spinning about him, he would only have needed an instantaneous burst of vision to have wondered who had submitted to whom.

He dreamed with his eyes open by the balcony lashed by the rain until a little after four. Then he bathed, put on his field uniform, and went down to the hotel to have breakfast. Later he made a routine inspection at the barracks, and suddenly he found himself standing on a corner with his hands in his pockets and not knowing what to do.

The owner of the poolroom saw him enter at dusk, with his hands still in his pockets. He greeted him from the back of the empty establishment, but the mayor didn't answer.

"A bottle of mineral water," he said.

The bottles made a loud noise as they were shifted about in the cooler.

"One of these days," the proprietor said, "they're going to have to operate on you and they'll find your liver all full of bubbles."

The mayor looked at the glass. He took a sip, belched, and remained with his elbows on the bar and his eyes fixed on the glass, and he belched again. The square was deserted.

"Well," the mayor said. "What's the matter?"

"It's Sunday," the proprietor said.

"Oh!"

He put a coin on the table and left without saying goodbye. On the corner of the square, someone who was walking as if he were dragging an enormous tail told him something that he didn't understand. A moment later he reacted. In a confused way he understood that something was going on and he went to the barracks. He bounded up the stairs without paying attention to the groups that were forming by the door. A policeman came out to meet him. He gave him a piece of paper and he needed only a glance to see what it was all about.

"He was handing it out at the cockpit," the policeman said.

The mayor ran down the hall. He opened the first cell and remained with his hand on the latch, scrutinizing the shadows until he was able to see: it was a boy of about twenty, with a sharp and sallow pockmarked face. He was wearing a baseball cap and glasses with broken lenses.

"What's your name?"

"Pepe."

"Pepe what?"

"Pepe Amador."

The mayor observed him for a moment and made an effort to remember. The boy was sitting on the concrete platform that served the prisoners as a bed. He seemed calm. He took off his glasses, cleaned them with his shirttail, and squinted at the mayor.

"Where have we seen each other?" the mayor asked.

"Around," said Pepe Amador.

The mayor didn't step into the cell. He kept looking at the prisoner, pensive, and then he started to shut the door.

"Well, Pepe," he said, "I think you fucked yourself up."

He turned the key, put it in his pocket, and went to the waiting room to read and reread the clandestine flier.

He sat down by the open balcony, slapping mosquitoes, while the lights in the deserted streets went on. He knew that sunset peace. At another time, during a sunset like that, he'd had the feeling of power in its fullness.

"So they've come back," he said to himself, aloud.

They'd come back. As before, they were mimeographed on both sides, and they could have been recognized anywhere and at any time by the indefinable mark of hesitation that clandestinity imprints.

He thought for a long time in the shadows, folding and unfolding the piece of paper before making a decision. Finally he put it in his pocket and felt for the keys to the cell.

"Rovira," he called.

The man he could trust came out of the darkness. The mayor gave him the keys.

"Take charge of that boy," he said. "Try to convince him to give you the names of the ones bringing clandestine propaganda into town. If you can't get them in a nice way," he made clear, "try any way you can to get him to talk."

The policeman reminded him that he was on patrol that night.

"Forget about it," the mayor said. "Don't worry about anything until you get new orders. And another thing," he added as if obeying an inspiration. "Send those men in the courtyard away. There won't be any patrols tonight."

He called to his armored office the three men who on his orders remained inactive in the barracks. He had them put on the uniforms he kept locked up in the closet. While they were doing that, he gathered on the table the blank cartridges that he'd issued to the men on patrol on previous nights and took a handful of live ammunition out of the safe.

"Tonight you people are going to do the patrolling," he told them, inspecting the rifles so that they'd have the best ones. "You don't have to do anything except let the people know that you're the ones who are on the street." Once they were all armed, he issued the ammunition. He stood in front of them.

"But listen well to one thing," he warned them. "The first one who does something foolish I'll have shot against the courtyard wall." He waited for a reaction that didn't come. "Understood?"

The three men—two Indian-looking, of ordinary appearance, and a blond with a tendency toward gigantism and eyes of transparent blue—had listened to the last words as they put bullets into the chambers. They came to attention.

"Understood, Lieutenant, sir."

"And something else," the mayor said, changing to an informal tone. "The Asíses are in town and it wouldn't be at all surprising if you ran into one of them, drunk and looking for some mess to get into. No matter what happens, don't get involved with him." Nor did he get the expected reaction that time either. "Understood?"

"Understood, Lieutenant, sir."

"Then you all know," the mayor concluded. "Keep your five senses on the alert."

When he closed the church after rosary, which he had moved up an hour because of the curfew, Father Ángel got a whiff of the smell of decay. It was a momentary stench, not enough to intrigue him. Later on, frying some slices of green plantain and warming milk for his meal, he found the cause of the smell: Trinidad, ill since Saturday, hadn't removed the dead mice. Then he returned to the church, opened and cleaned out the traps, and then went to Mina's, two blocks from the church.

Toto Visbal himself opened the door. In the small dark parlor, where there were several leather stools in disorder and prints hanging on the walls, Mina's mother and her blind grandmother were drinking something hot and aromatic in cups. Mina was making artificial flowers.

"It's been two weeks," the blind woman said, "that we haven't seen you in this house, Father."

It was true. Every afternoon he'd passed by the window where Mina was sitting making paper flowers, but he never went in.

"Time passes without making any noise," he said. And then, making it clear that he was in a hurry, he turned to Toto Visbal. "I've come to ask you to let Mina come and take charge of the traps starting tomorrow. Trinidad," he explained to Mina, "has been sick since Saturday."

Toto Visbal gave his consent.

"It's a wish to lose time," the blind woman put in. "After all's said and done, the world is coming to an end this year."

Mina's mother put a hand on her knee as a sign to be still. The blind woman pushed the hand away.

"God punishes superstition," the curate said.

"It's written," the blind woman said. "Blood will run in the streets and there won't be any human power capable of stopping it."

The priest gave her a look of pity: she was very old, extremely pale, and her dead eyes seemed to penetrate the secret of things.

"We'll be bathed in blood," Mina mocked.

Then Father Ángel turned to her. He saw her rise up, with her intensely black hair and the same paleness as the blind woman's, from amidst a confused swirl of ribbons and colored paper. She looked like an allegorical vignette at a school pageant.

"And you," he told her, "working on Sunday."

"I already told her," the blind woman put in. "Burning ashes will rain down on her head."

"Necessity has the face of a dog." Mina smiled.

Since the curate was still standing, Toto Visbal brought over a chair and invited him again to sit down. He was a fragile man, with startled movements because of his timidity.

"Thank you just the same." Father Ángel refused. "The curfew will catch me on the street." He noticed the deep silence in the town and commented: "It seems later than eight o'clock."

Then he found out: after almost two years of empty cells, Pepe Amador was in jail and the town at the mercy of three criminals. People had shut themselves up since six o'clock.

"It's strange." Father Ángel seemed to be talking to himself. "A thing getting out of hand like that."

"Sooner or later it had to happen," said Toto Visbal. "The whole country is patched up with cobwebs."

The priest continued to the door.

"Haven't you seen the clandestine fliers?"

Father Ángel stopped, perplexed.

"Again?"

"In August," the blind woman put in, "the three days of darkness will begin."

Mina reached out to give her a flower she'd begun. "Be still," she told her, "and stop that." The blind woman recognized the flower by touch.

"So they've come back," the priest said.

"About a week ago," said Toto Visbal. "Because there was one here, without anybody's knowing who brought it. You know what it's like."

The curate nodded.

"They say that everything's just the same as before," Toto Visbal went on. "The government changed, they promised peace and guarantees, and at first everybody believed them. But the officials are the same ones."

"And it's true," put in Mina's mother. "Here we are with the curfew again, and those three criminals on the street."

"But there's one thing new," Toto Visbal said. "Now they're saying that they're organizing guerrilla groups against the government in the interior again."

"That's all written down," the blind woman said.

"It's absurd," said the curate, pensive. "We have to recognize that the attitude has changed. Or at least," he corrected himself, "it had changed until tonight."

Hours later, lying awake in the heat of his mosquito netting, he wondered, nonetheless, whether in reality time had passed during the nineteen years he'd been in the parish.

Across from his very house he heard the noise of the boots and weapons that in different times had preceded rifle shots. Except this time the boots went away, passed by again an hour later, and went away once more without any shots being fired. A short while after, tormented by the fatigue of sleeplessness and the heat, he realized that the cocks had been crowing for some time.

$\mathcal{M}$ATEO ASÍS tried to calculate the hour by the location of the roosters. Finally he rose to the surface of reality.

"What time is it?"

Nora Jacob stretched out her arm in the shadows and picked up the clock with its phosphorescent dial from the night table. The answer, which she still hadn't given, woke her up completely.

"Four-thirty," she said.

"Shit!"

Mateo Asís jumped out of bed. But the pain in his head and then the mineral sediment in his mouth obliged him to moderate his drive. He felt with his feet in the darkness for his shoes.

"Daylight might have caught me," he said.

"How nice," she said. She turned on the small lamp and recognized his knotty spine and pale buttocks. "You'd have

151

had to stay shut up here until morning."

She was completely naked, only covering her sex with an edge of the sheet. Even her voice lost its warm impudence when the light was turned on.

Mateo Asís put on his shoes. He was tall and sturdy. Nora Jacob, who had received him occasionally for two years, felt a kind of frustration at the bad luck of having in secret a man who seemed to her to be made for a woman to talk about.

"If you don't watch out you're going to get fat," she said.

"It's the good life," he replied, trying to hide his displeasure. And he added, smiling: "I must be pregnant."

"I wish you were," she said. "If men gave birth, they'd be less inconsiderate."

Mateo Asís picked the condom up off the floor with his underdrawers, went to the bathroom, and threw it into the toilet. He washed, trying not to breathe deeply: at dawn any smell was her smell. When he went back into the room he found her sitting up in bed.

"One of these days," Nora Jacob said, "I'm going to get tired of this hiding and I'm going to tell the whole world."

He didn't look at her until he was completely dressed. She became aware of her firm breasts and without stopping talking she covered herself up to the neck with the sheet.

"I can't see the time," she went on, "so let's have breakfast in bed and stay here until afternoon. I'm capable of putting up a lampoon myself."

He gave a broad laugh.

"Little old Benjamín would die," he said. "How's that going?"

"You can imagine," she said. "Waiting for Néstor Jacob to die."

She saw him wave goodbye from the door. "Try to make it back on Christmas Eve," she told him. He promised. He tiptoed across the courtyard and went out into the street through the main door. There was an icy dew that just dampened the skin. A shout came up to meet him as he reached the square.

"Halt!"

A flashlight was turned on into his eyes. He averted his face.

"Oh, shit!" the mayor said, invisible behind the light. "Look what we've found. Are you coming or going?"

He turned off the flashlight and Mateo Asís saw him, accompanied by three policemen. His face was fresh and washed and he had the submachine gun slung.

"Coming," said Mateo Asís.

The mayor came forward to look at his watch in the light of the street lamp. There were ten minutes left till five. With a signal directed at the policemen, he ordered an end to the curfew. He remained in suspension until the end of the bugle call, which put a sad note into the dawn. Then he sent the policemen away and accompanied Mateo Asís across the square.

"That's that," he said. "The mess with the papers is over."

More than satisfaction, there was weariness in his voice.

"Did they catch the one who was doing it?"

"Not yet," the mayor said. "But I just made the last rounds and I can assure you that today, for the first time, not a single piece of paper will see the light of dawn. It was a matter of tying up their pants."

On reaching the main door of his house, Mateo Asís went ahead to tie up the dogs. The servant women were starting to move about in the kitchen. When the mayor entered he was greeted by an uproar of chained dogs, which, a moment later, was replaced by the steps and sighs of peaceful animals. The widow Asís found them sitting and drinking coffee on the stone bench in the kitchen. It had grown light.

"An early-rising man," the widow said, "a good spouse but a bad husband."

In spite of her good humor, her face revealed the mortification of an intense night vigil. The mayor answered her greeting. He picked the submachine gun off the floor and slung it over his shoulder.

"Drink all the coffee you want, Lieutenant," the widow said, "but don't bring any shotguns into my house."

"On the contrary." Mateo Asís smiled. "You should borrow it to go to mass with. Don't you think?"

"I don't need junk like that to defend myself," the widow replied. "Divine Providence is on our side. The Asíses," she added seriously, "were people of God before there were priests for many miles around."

The mayor took his leave. "I've got to get some sleep," he said. "This is no life for a Christian." He made his way among the hens and ducks and turkeys who were beginning to invade the house. The widow Asís shooed the animals away. Mateo Asís went to his room, bathed, changed clothes, and went out again to saddle up his mule. His brothers had left at dawn.

The widow Asís was taking care of the cages when her son appeared in the courtyard.

"Remember," she told him, "it's one thing to look after your hide and something else to know how to keep your distance."

"He only came to have a mug of coffee," Mateo Asís said. "We walked along talking, almost without realizing it."

He was at the end of the porch, looking at his mother, but she hadn't turned when she spoke. She seemed to be addressing the birds. "I'm just going to tell you this," she replied. "Don't bring any murderers into my house." Having finished with the cages, she occupied herself entirely with her son:

"And you, where have you been?"

That morning Judge Arcadio thought he'd discovered ominous signs in the minute episodes that make up daily life. "It gives you a headache," he said, trying to explain his uneasiness to his wife. It was a sunny morning. The river, for the first time in several weeks, had lost its menacing look and its raw-meat smell. Judge Arcadio went to the barbershop.

"Justice," the barber received him, "limps along, but it gets there all the same."

The floor had been oiled and the mirrors were covered with brushstrokes of white lead. The barber began to polish them with a rag while Judge Arcadio settled into the chair.

"There shouldn't be such things as Mondays," the judge said.

The barber had begun to cut his hair.

"It's all Sunday's fault," he said. "If it weren't for Sunday," he stated with a merry air, "there wouldn't be any Mondays."

Judge Arcadio closed his eyes. That time, after ten hours of sleep, a turbulent act of love, and a prolonged bath, there was nothing to reproach Sunday for. But it was a thick Monday. When the clock in the tower struck nine and in place of the pealing of the bell there was the hiss of a sewing machine next door, another sign made Judge Arcadio shudder: the silence in the streets.

"This is a ghost town," he said.

"You people wanted it that way," the barber said. "Before, on a Monday morning, I would have cut at least five heads of hair by now. Today God's first gift to me is you."

Judge Arcadio opened his eyes and for a moment contemplated the river in the mirror. "You people," he repeated. And he asked:

"Who are we?"

"You people." The barber hesitated. "Before you people this was a shitty town, like all of them, but now it's the worst of them all."

"If you're telling me these things," the judge replied, "it's because you know I haven't had anything to do with them. Would you dare," he asked without being aggressive, "say the same thing to the lieutenant?"

The barber admitted he wouldn't.

"You don't know what it's like," he said, "getting up every morning with the certainty that they're going to kill you and ten years pass without their killing you."

"I don't know," Judge Arcadio admitted, "and I don't want to know."

"Do everything possible," the barber said, "so that you'll never know."

The judge lowered his head. After a prolonged silence, he asked: "Do you know something, Guardiola?" Without waiting for an answer he went on: "The lieutenant is sinking deep into this town. And he sinks in deeper every day because he's discovered a pleasure from which there's no turning back: little by little, without making a lot of noise, he's getting rich." Since the barber was listening to him in silence, he concluded:

"I'll bet you that he won't be responsible for a single death more."

"Do you think so?"

"I'll bet you a hundred to one," Judge Arcadio insisted. "At this moment there's no better business for him than peace."

The barber finished cutting his hair, tilted the chair back, and shifted the sheet without speaking. When he finally did, there was a thread of uneasiness in his voice.

"It's strange that you should be the one to say that," he said, "and to say it to me."

If his position had allowed it, Judge Arcadio would have shrugged his shoulders.

"It's not the first time I've said it," he stated.

"The lieutenant's your best friend," the barber said.

He'd lowered his voice and it was tense and confidential. Concentrating on his work, he had the same expression a person not in the habit of writing has when he signs his name.

"Tell me one thing, Guardiola," Judge Arcadio asked with a certain solemnity. "What impression do you have of me?"

The barber had begun to shave him. He thought for a moment before answering.

"Until now," he said, "I'd have thought that you're a man who knows that he's leaving and wants to leave."

"You can keep on thinking that." The judge smiled.

He let himself be shaved with the same gloomy passivity with which he would have let his throat be cut. He kept his eyes closed while the barber rubbed his jaw with a piece of alum, powdered him, and brushed off the powder with a very soft brush. When he took the sheet from around his neck, he slipped a piece of paper into his shirt pocket.

"You're only mistaken about one thing, Judge," he told him. "There's going to be a great big mess in this country."

Judge Arcadio checked to see that they were still alone in the barbershop. The burning sun, the hiss of the sewing machine in the nine-thirty silence, the unavoidable Monday, indicated something more to him: they seemed to be alone in the town. Then he took the piece of paper out of his pocket and read it.

The barber turned his back to him and put his shelf in order. " 'Two years of speeches,' " he quoted from memory. " 'And still the same state of siege, the same censorship of the press, the same old officials.' " On seeing in the mirror that Judge Arcadio had stopped reading, he told him:

"Pass it around."

The judge put the paper back in his pocket.

"You're very brave," he said.

"If I'd ever made a mistake about anybody," the barber said, "I'd have been full of lead years ago." Then he added in a serious voice, "And remember one thing, Judge. Nobody's going to be able to stop it this time."

When he left the barbershop, Judge Arcadio felt his palate was all dry. He asked for two double shots at the poolroom, and after drinking them, one after the other, he saw that he still had a lot of time to kill. At the university, one Holy Saturday, he'd tried to apply a jackass cure to uncertainty: he went into the toilet of a bar, perfectly sober, threw some gunpowder on a chancre, and lighted it.

With the fourth drink, Don Roque moderated the dosage. "At this rate"—he smiled—"they'll carry you out on their shoulders like a bullfighter." He, too, smiled with his lips, but his eyes were still extinguished. A half hour later he went to the toilet, urinated, and before leaving flushed the clandestine note down the toilet.

When he got back to the bar he found the bottle next to the glass, the level of the contents marked with a line in ink. "That's all for you," Don Roque told him, fanning himself slowly. They were alone in the place. Judge Arcadio poured himself half a glass and began to drink slowly. "Do you know something?" he asked. And since Don Roque showed no signs of having understood, he told him:

"There's going to be a great big mess."

Don Sabas was weighing his bird breakfast on the scale when he was told of another visit by Mr. Carmichael. "Tell him I'm sleeping," he whispered into his wife's ear. And indeed, ten minutes later he was asleep. When he awoke, the air had become dry again and the house was paralyzed with the heat. It was after twelve.

"What did you dream about?" his wife asked.

"Nothing."

She'd waited for her husband to awaken without being roused. A moment later she boiled the hypodermic syringe and Don Sabas gave himself an injection of insulin in the thigh.

"It's been about three years now that you haven't dreamed anything," his wife said with slow disenchantment.

"God damn it," he exclaimed. "What do you want now? A person can't be forced to dream."

Years before, in a brief midday dream, Don Sabas had dreamed of an oak tree which, instead of flowers, bore razor blades. His wife interpreted the dream and won a piece of the lottery.

"If not today, tomorrow," she said.

"It wasn't today and it won't be tomorrow," Don Sabas replied impatiently. "I'm not going to dream just so you can act like a jackass."

He stretched out again on the bed while his wife put the room in order. All types of cutting or stabbing instruments had been banished from the room. When a half hour had passed, Don Sabas arose in varying tempos, trying not to excite himself, and began to dress.

"So," he asked then, "what did Carmichael say?"

"That he'll be back later."

They didn't speak again until they were sitting at the table. Don Sabas picked at his uncomplicated sick man's diet. She served herself a full lunch, at first sight too abundant for her fragile body and languid expression. She'd thought it over a lot before she decided to ask:

"What is it that Carmichael wants?"

Don Sabas didn't even lift his head.

"Money. What else?"

"I thought so," the woman sighed. And she went on piously: "Poor Carmichael, rivers of money passing through his hands for so many years and living off public charity." As she spoke, she lost her enthusiasm for lunch.

"Give it to him, Sabitas," she begged. "God will reward you." She crossed her knife and fork over the plate and asked, intrigued: "How much does he need?"

"Two hundred pesos," Don Sabas answered imperturbably.

"Two hundred pesos!"

"Just imagine!"

Completely unlike Sunday, which was his busiest day, Don Sabas had a peaceful afternoon on Mondays. He could spend long hours in his office, dozing in front of the electric fan while the cattle grew, fattened, and multiplied on his ranches. That afternoon, however, he couldn't manage an instant of rest.

"It's the heat," the woman said.

Don Sabas let a spark of exasperation be seen in his faded eyes. In the narrow office, with an old wooden desk, four leather easy chairs, and harnesses piled in the corners, the blinds had been drawn and the air was warm and thick.

"It could be," he said. "It's never been this hot in October."

"Fifteen years ago, when there was heat like this, there

was an earthquake," his wife said. "Do you remember?"

"I don't remember," said Don Sabas distractedly. "You know that I never remember anything. Besides," he added grouchily, "I'm in no mood to talk about misfortunes this afternoon."

Closing his eyes, his arms crossed over his stomach, he feigned sleep. "If Carmichael comes," he murmured, "tell him I'm not in." An expression of entreaty altered his wife's face.

"You're in a bad mood," she said.

But he didn't speak again. She left the office without making the slightest sound as she closed the screen door. Toward dusk, after having really slept, Don Sabas opened his eyes and in front of him, like the prolongation of a dream, he saw the mayor waiting for him to wake up.

"A man like you"—the lieutenant smiled—"shouldn't sleep with the door open."

Don Sabas showed no expression that could reveal his upset. "For you," he said, "the doors of my house are always open." He reached out his hand to ring the bell, but the mayor stopped him with a gesture.

"Don't you want some coffee?" Don Sabas asked.

"Not right now," the mayor said, looking over the room with a nostalgic glance. "It was very nice here while you were asleep. It was like being in a different town."

Don Sabas rubbed his eyelids with the back of his fingers.

"What time is it?"

The mayor looked at his watch. "It's going on five," he said. Then, changing his position in the chair, he softly went into what he wanted to say.

"So shall we talk?"

"I suppose," said Don Sabas, "that I've got very little choice."

"It wouldn't be worth the trouble not to," the mayor

said. "After all, this isn't a secret to anybody." And with the same restful fluidity, without forcing his gestures or his words at any moment, he added:

"Tell me one thing, Don Sabas: how many head of cattle belonging to the widow Montiel have you had cut out and branded with your mark since she offered to sell to you?"

Don Sabas shrugged his shoulders.

"I haven't got the slightest idea."

"You remember," the mayor stated, "that a thing like that has a name."

"Rustling." Don Sabas was precise.

"That's right," the mayor confirmed. "Let us say, for example," he went on without changing his tone, "that you've cut out two hundred head in three days."

"I wish I had," Don Sabas said.

"Two hundred, let's say," the mayor said. "You know what the conditions are: fifty pesos a head in municipal tax."

"Forty."

"Fifty."

Don Sabas made a pause of resignation. He was leaning against the back of the swivel chair, turning the ring with the polished black stone on his finger, his eyes fixed on an imaginary chessboard.

The mayor was observing him with an attention completely devoid of pity. "This time, however, things don't stop there," he went on. "From this moment on, wherever they might be, all cattle belonging to the estate of José Montiel are under the protection of the town government." Having waited uselessly for a reaction, he explained:

"That poor woman, as you know, is completely mad."

"What about Carmichael?"

"Carmichael," the mayor said, "has been in custody for two hours."

Don Sabas examined him then with an expression that could have been one of devotion or one of stupor. And without any warning, the bland and voluminous body exploded over the desk, shaken by uncontainable interior laughter.

"What a miracle, Lieutenant," he said. "This all must seem like a dream to you."

At dusk Dr. Giraldo possessed the certainty of having gained much ground on the past. The almond trees on the square were dusty again. A new winter was passing, but its stealthy footprints were leaving a profound imprint in his memory. Father Ángel was returning from his afternoon walk when he found the doctor trying to put his key into the lock of his office.

"You see, Doctor." He smiled. "Even to open a door you need the help of God."

"Or a flashlight." The doctor smiled in turn.

He turned the key in the lock and then gave all his attention to Father Ángel. He saw him thick and hazy in the dusk. "Wait a moment, Father," he said. "I don't think everything's working right with your liver." He held him by the arm.

"You don't think so?"

The doctor turned on the light by the doorway and with an attention more personal than professional examined the curate's face. Then he opened the screen door and turned on the light in the office.

"It wouldn't be too much to devote five minutes to your body, Father," he said. "Let's have a look at that blood pressure."

Father Ángel was in a hurry. But at the doctor's insistence he went into the office and prepared his arm for the sphygmomanometer.

"In my time," he said, "those things didn't exist."

Dr. Giraldo put a chair in front of him and sat down to apply the sphygmomanometer.

"This is your time, Father." He smiled. "Your body won't let you out of it."

While the doctor was studying the dial, the curate examined the room with that boobish curiosity that consulting rooms tend to inspire. Hanging on the walls were a yellowing diploma, the print of a ruddy-faced girl with one cheek eaten away in blue, and the painting of a doctor fighting with death over a naked woman. In the back, behind the white iron cot, there was a cabinet with labeled bottles. Beside the window a glass cabinet with instruments and two others crammed with books. The only smell that could be defined was that of denatured alcohol.

Dr. Giraldo's face didn't reveal anything when he finished taking the blood pressure.

"You need a saint in this room," Father Ángel murmured.

The doctor examined the walls. "Not just here," he said. "He's needed all over town." He put the sphygmomanometer away in a leather case and closed it with an energetic tug on the zipper, and said:

"You ought to know one thing, Father: your blood pressure's fine."

"I imagined so," the curate said. And he added with a languid perplexity: "I never felt better in October."

He slowly began to roll his sleeve down. With his cassock with darned edges, his cracked shoes, and the harsh hands with nails that were like singed horn, at that instant his essential condition prevailed: he was an extremely poor man.

"Still," the doctor replied, "I'm worried about you. You have to recognize that your daily routine isn't the best for an October like this one."

"Our Lord is demanding," the priest said.

The doctor turned his back to him to look at the dark river through the window. "I wonder to what point," he said. "It doesn't seem to be God's work, this business of trying so hard for so many years to cover people's instinct with armor, knowing full well that underneath it all everything goes on the same." And after a long pause he asked:

"Haven't you had the impression that during the last few days his implacable work has begun to fall apart?"

"Every night for all of my life I've had that impression," Father Ángel said. "That's why I know that I've got to begin with more strength the next day."

He had stood up. "It's going on six," he said, getting ready to leave the doctor's office. Without moving from the window, the doctor seemed to put an arm in his path to tell him:

"Father: one of these nights put your hand on your heart and ask yourself if you're not trying to put bandages on morality."

Father Ángel couldn't hide a terrible inner suffocation. "At the hour of death," he said, "you'll learn how heavy those words are, Doctor." He said good night and softly closed the door as he left.

He couldn't concentrate on his prayers. When he was closing up the church, Mina came over to tell him that only one mouse had fallen in two days. He had the impression that with Trinidad's absence the mice had proliferated to the point of threatening to undermine the church. Still, Mina had set the traps. She'd poisoned the cheese, followed the trail of the young ones, and plugged up the new nests that he himself helped her to find with tar.

"Put a little faith into your work," he'd told her, "and the mice will come into the traps like lambs."

He gave a lot of turns on the bare mattress before falling

asleep. In the enervation of wakefulness he became fully aware of the obscure feeling of defeat that the doctor had implanted in his heart. That disquiet, and then the troop of mice in the church and the frightful paralysis of the curfew, all plotted so that a blind force would drag him into the turbulence of his most fearsome memory:

Having just arrived in town, he'd been awakened in the middle of the night to give the last rites to Nora Jacob. He'd received a dramatic confession, given in a serene way, concise and detailed, in a bedroom prepared to receive death: all that remained were a crucifix at the head of the bed and several empty chairs against the walls. The dying woman had revealed to him that her husband, Néstor Jacob, was not the father of the daughter who had just been born. Father Ángel had conditioned absolution on her repeating the confession and finishing the act of contrition in the presence of her husband.

OBEYING the rhythmic orders of the impresario, the gangs pulled up the stakes and the canvas deflated in a solemn catastrophe, with a moaning whistle like that of the wind in the trees. By dawn it was folded up and the women and children were eating breakfast among the trunks, while the men put the wild animals on board. When the launches gave their first whistle, the marks left by the bonfires on the vacant lot were the only sign that a prehistoric animal had passed through the town.

The mayor hadn't slept. After watching the loading of the circus from the balcony, he mingled in the turmoil of the port, still wearing his field uniform, his eyes irritated from lack of sleep, and his face hardened by a two-day beard. The impresario spotted him from the roof of the launch.

"Hello, Lieutenant," he shouted to him. "I leave you your kingdom there."

He was wrapped in ample and worn overalls, which gave his round face a priestly air. He carried the whip rolled in his fist.

The mayor went over to the edge of the dock. "I'm sorry, General," he shouted good-humoredly in turn, his arms open. "I hope that you'll be honest enough to tell them why you're leaving." He turned to the crowd and explained in a loud voice:

"I revoked his license because he refused to give a free performance for the children."

The final whistle of the launches and the noise of the engines drowned out the impresario's reply. The water exhaled a breath of stirred mud. The impresario waited until the launches had made their turn in the middle of the river. Then he leaned over the rail and using his hands as a megaphone, he shouted with all the power of his lungs:

"Goodbye, you son-of-a-bitch cop."

The mayor didn't react. He waited, his hands in his pockets, until the sound of the engines disappeared. Then he made his way through the crowd, smiling, and went into Moisés the Syrian's shop.

It was almost eight o'clock. The Syrian had begun to put away the merchandise exhibited by the door.

"So you're leaving too," the mayor said to him.

"In a little while," the Syrian said, looking at the sky, "it's going to rain."

"It doesn't rain on Wednesdays," the mayor stated.

He leaned his elbows on the counter, observing the thick clouds that floated over the docks until the Syrian finished putting away the merchandise and told his wife to bring them some coffee.

"At this rate"—he sighed as if to himself—"we'll have to get people on loan from other towns."

The mayor drank his coffee with spaced sips. Three more

families had left town. With them, according to Moisés the Syrian's calculations, it made five that had left in one week.

"Sooner or later they'll be back," the mayor said. He scrutinized the enigmatic marks left by the coffee in the bottom of the cup and commented with an absent air: "Wherever they go, they'll remember that their umbilical cords are buried in this town."

In spite of his prognostication, he had to wait in the store for the passing of a violent cloudburst that sank the town into a deluge for a few minutes. Then he went to the police barracks and found Mr. Carmichael, still sitting on a stool in the center of the courtyard, soaked by the downpour.

He paid no attention to him. After receiving the report from the policeman on guard, he had them open the cell where Pepe Amador seemed to be in a deep sleep face down on the brick floor. He turned him over with his foot and for a moment observed with secret pity the face disfigured by the blows.

"How long since he's eaten?" he asked.

"Since night before last."

He ordered them to pick him up. Dragging him by the armpits, three policemen hauled the body through the cell and sat it on the concrete platform jutting from the wall at a height of two feet. In the place where his body had been, a damp shadow remained.

While two policemen held him sitting up, another supported his head by grasping the hair. One would have thought that he was dead but for the irregular breathing and the expression of infinite weariness on his lips.

On being abandoned by the policemen, Pepe Amador opened his eyes, gripped the edge of the concrete by feel. Then he lay down on the platform with a hoarse moan.

The mayor left the cell and ordered them to give him something to eat and let him sleep awhile. "Then," he said, "keep working on him until he spits up everything he knows. I don't think he'll be able to resist for long." From the balcony he saw Mr. Carmichael in the courtyard, his face in his hands, huddled on the stool.

"Rovira," he called. "Go to Carmichael's house and tell his wife to send him some clothes. Then," he added in a peremptory way, "bring him to the office."

He'd begun to fall asleep, leaning on the desk, when they knocked on the door. It was Mr. Carmichael, dressed in white and completely dry, with the exception of the shoes, which were swollen and soft like those of a drowned man. Before dealing with him, the mayor ordered the policeman to come back with a pair of shoes.

Mr. Carmichael raised an arm toward the policeman. "I'm all right this way," he said. And then, addressing the mayor with a look of severe dignity, he explained:

"These are the only ones I own."

The mayor had him sit down. Twenty-four hours earlier Mr. Carmichael had been led into the armored office and subjected to an intense interrogation concerning the situation of the Montiel estate. He had given a detailed exposition. Finally, when the mayor revealed his proposal to buy the estate at a price fixed by municipal experts, he had announced his inflexible determination not to permit it until the will had been probated.

That afternoon, after two days of hunger and exposure to the elements, his reply revealed the same inflexibility.

"You're a mule, Carmichael," the mayor told him. "If you wait for the will to be probated, that bandit Don Sabas will have put his brand on all the Montiel cattle."

Mr. Carmichael shrugged his shoulders.

"All right," the mayor said after a long pause. "We all know that you're an honest man. But remember one thing: five years ago Don Sabas gave José Montiel the complete list of the people in contact with the guerrilla groups, and that's why he was the only leader of the opposition who could remain in town."

"Another one stayed," Mr. Carmichael said with a touch of sarcasm. "The dentist."

The mayor ignored the interruption.

"Do you think that a man like that, capable of selling out his own people, is going to care if you've been sitting outside for twenty-four hours rain or shine?"

Mr. Carmichael lowered his head and began to look at his nails. The mayor sat on the desk.

"Besides," he said finally in a soft tone, "think about your children."

Mr. Carmichael didn't know that his wife and his two oldest children had visited the mayor the night before and he had promised them that he'd be released within twenty-four hours.

"Don't worry," Mr. Carmichael said. "They know how to take care of themselves."

He didn't lift his head until he heard the mayor walking from one end of the office to the other. Then he gave a sigh and said: "You still have another way out, Lieutenant." Before continuing, he looked at him with soft gentleness:

"Shoot me."

He didn't receive any reply. A moment later the mayor was sleeping deeply in his room and Mr. Carmichael had gone back to the stool.

Only two blocks away from the barracks, the secretary of the court was happy. He'd spent the morning dozing in the back of the office, and without being able to avoid it, he'd seen the splendid breasts of Rebeca Asís. It was like a lightning flash at noon: suddenly the door of the bathroom had opened and the fascinating woman, with nothing on but a towel wrapped around her head, gave a silent shout and hurried to close the window.

For half an hour the secretary went on suffering the bitterness of that hallucination in the half light of the office. Toward twelve o'clock he put the padlock on the door and went to feed his memory something.

As he passed by the telegraph office, the postmaster signaled to him. "We're going to have a new priest," he told him. "The widow Asís wrote a letter to the apostolic prefect." The secretary waved him off.

"The greatest virtue in a man," he said, "is knowing how to keep a secret."

On the corner of the square he ran into Mr. Benjamín, who was thinking twice before leaping over the puddles in front of his store. "If you only knew, Mr. Benjamín," the secretary began.

"What?" asked Mr. Benjamín.

"Nothing," the secretary said. "I'll carry this secret with me to the grave."

Mr. Benjamín shrugged his shoulders. He watched the secretary leap over the puddles with such a youthful agility that he, too, threw himself into the adventure.

In his absence someone had placed a lunch carrier in three sections, plates, and silverware, and a folded tablecloth, in the rear of the store. Mr. Benjamín spread out the cloth on the table and put the things in order to have lunch. He did everything with extreme neatness. First he had the soup, yellow, with a large circle of grease floating, and a stripped bone. On another plate he ate white rice, roasted meat, and a piece of fried cassava. The heat was starting up, but Mr. Benjamín paid no attention to it. When he'd finished lunch, having piled up the plates and put the sections of the lunch carrier in place, he drank a glass of water. He was getting ready to hang up his hammock when he heard someone coming into the store.

A sleepy voice asked:

"Is Mr. Benjamín here?"

He stuck out his neck and saw a woman dressed in black with her hair wrapped in a towel and ash-colored skin. It was Pepe Amador's mother.

"I'm not in," Mr. Benjamín said.

"It's you," the woman said.

"I know," he said, "but it's just as if I weren't because I know why you're looking for me."

The woman hesitated by the small door to the rear of the shop, while Mr. Benjamín finished putting up the hammock. With every breath a thin whistle escaped from her lungs.

"Don't stand there," Mr. Benjamín said harshly. "Go away or come in."

The woman occupied the chair by the table and began to sob in silence.

"Excuse me," he said. "You have to realize that you compromise me by standing there in sight of everybody."

Pepe Amador's mother uncovered her head and dried her eyes with the towel. Out of pure habit, Mr. Benjamín tested the resistance of the ropes when he finished putting up the hammock. Then he saw to the woman.

"So," he said, "you want me to write you a writ."

The woman nodded.

"That's right," Mr. Benjamín went on. "You go right on believing in writs. These days," he explained, lowering his voice, "justice doesn't depend on writs; it depends on bullets."

"Everybody says the same thing," she answered, "but the fact is that I'm the only one whose boy is in jail."

While she was talking she undid the knots on the handkerchief she'd been holding in her fist until then, and took out a few sweaty bills: eight pesos. She offered them to Mr. Benjamín.

"It's all I've got."

Mr. Benjamín observed the money. He shrugged his shoulders, took the bills, and laid them on the table. "I know it's useless," he said. "But I'm going to do it just to prove to God that I'm a stubborn man." The woman thanked him silently and began weeping again.

"In any case," Mr. Benjamín advised her, "try to get the mayor to let you see the boy and convince him to tell what he knows. Without that it would be like throwing writs to the hogs."

She wiped her nose with the towel, covered her head again, and left the store without turning her face.

Mr. Benjamín slept his siesta until four o'clock. When he went into the courtyard to wash, the weather had cleared and the air was full of flying ants. After changing his clothes and combing the few threads of hair he had left, he went to the telegraph office to buy a sheet of stamped paper.

He was coming back to the store to write the writ when he saw that something was happening in town. He heard distant shouts. He asked a group of boys who ran past him what was going on, and they answered without stopping. Then he went back to the telegraph office and returned the sheet of stamped paper.

"I don't need it now," he said. "They've just killed Pepe Amador."

Still half asleep, carrying his belt in one hand and buttoning his tunic with the other, the mayor went down the steps from his bedroom in two leaps. The color of the light mixed up his sense of time. He understood before he knew what was going on that he had to go to the barracks.

The windows were being closed as he passed. A woman

with her arms open came along in the middle of the street, running in the opposite direction. There were flying ants in the clean air. Still not knowing what was going on, the mayor unholstered his revolver and started to run.

A group of women was trying to force the door of the barracks. Several men were struggling with them to keep them out. The mayor beat them away, put his back against the door, and aimed at all of them.

"I'll drop anyone who takes a step."

A policeman who'd been holding it from inside then opened the door, with his rifle at the ready, and blew his whistle. Two other policemen ran out onto the balcony, fired several shots in the air, and the group scattered to the ends of the street. At that moment, howling like a dog, the woman appeared on the corner. The mayor recognized Pepe Amador's mother. He gave a leap inside the barracks and from the stairway ordered the policeman:

"Take charge of that woman."

Inside there was complete silence. The mayor really didn't find out what had happened until he moved aside the policemen who were blocking the entrance to the cell and saw Pepe Amador. Lying on the floor, curled up, he had his hands between his thighs. He was pale, but there were no signs of blood.

After convincing himself that there was no wound, the mayor laid the body out face up, tucked in the shirttail, and buttoned the fly. Finally he fastened the belt.

When he stood up he'd recovered his calm, but the expression with which he faced the policemen revealed a beginning of weariness.

"Who did it?"

"All of us," the blond giant said. "He tried to escape."

The mayor looked at him thoughtfully, and for a few seconds seemed not to have anything else to say. "Nobody's going to buy that story," he said. He advanced toward the blond giant with his hand outstretched.

"Give me your revolver."

The policeman took off his belt and handed it over. Having replaced the two spent shells with new rounds, the mayor put them in his pocket and gave the revolver to another policeman. The blond giant, who, seen from close by, seemed illuminated by an aura of childishness, let himself be led to the next cell. There he got completely undressed and gave his clothes to the mayor. Everything was done unhurriedly, each one knowing the action that corresponded to him, as in a ceremony. Finally the mayor himself closed the dead man's cell and went out onto the courtyard balcony. Mr. Carmichael was still on the stool.

Led to the office, he didn't respond to the invitation to sit down. He remained standing in front of the desk, with his clothes wet once more, and he barely moved his head when the mayor asked him if he'd been aware of everything.

"Well, then," the mayor said. "I still haven't had time to think about what I'm going to do, or even if I'm going to do anything. But no matter what I do," he added, "remember this: like it or not, you're in on the deal."

Mr. Carmichael remained absorbed in front of the desk, his clothes sticking to his body and a beginning of tumefaction in his skin, as if he still hadn't floated to the surface on his third night as a drowned man. The mayor waited uselessly for a sign of life.

"So take the situation into account, Carmichael: we're partners now."

He said it gravely and even with a touch of drama. But Mr. Carmichael's brain didn't seem to register it. He remained motionless facing the desk, swollen and sad, even after the armored door had closed.

In front of the barracks two policemen held Pepe Amador's mother by the wrists. The three seemed to be at rest. The woman was breathing with a peaceful rhythm and her eyes were dry. But when the mayor appeared in the door she gave off a hoarse howl and shook with such violence that one of the policemen had to let her go and the other one pinned her to the ground with a wrestling hold.

The mayor didn't look at her. Bringing the other policeman with him, he confronted the group that was witnessing the struggle from the corner. He didn't address anyone in particular.

"Someone of you," he said. "If you want to avoid something worse, take this woman home."

Still accompanied by the policeman, he made his way through the group and reached the courthouse. He found nobody there. Then he went to Judge Arcadio's house and pushing open the door without knocking, he shouted:

"Judge."

Judge Arcadio's wife, overwhelmed by the thick humors of her pregnancy, answered in the shadows.

"He left."

The mayor didn't move from the threshold.

"For where?"

"Where else would he go?" the woman said. "Some shitty whore place."

The mayor signaled the policeman to go in. They passed by the woman without looking at her. After turning the bedroom upside down and realizing that there weren't any men's things anywhere, they went back into the living room.

"When did he leave?" the mayor asked.

"Two nights ago," the woman said.

The mayor needed a long pause to think.

"That son of a bitch," he suddenly shouted. "He can hide a hundred feet underground, he can crawl back into the belly of his whore mother, but we'll haul him out dead or alive. The government has a very long arm."

The woman sighed.

"May God listen to you, Lieutenant."

It was beginning to grow dark. There were still groups being kept at a distance by policemen at the corners of the barracks, but they'd taken Pepe Amador's mother home and the town seemed peaceful.

The mayor went straight to the dead man's cell. He had them bring a piece of canvas and, aided by the policeman, he put the cap and glasses on the corpse and wrapped it up. Then he looked in different parts of the barracks for pieces of cord and wire and tied the body in a spiral from neck to ankles. When he finished he was sweating, but he had a recovered look. It was as if physically he had gotten rid of the weight of the corpse.

Only then did he turn on the light in the cell. "Get the shovel, the pick, and a lantern," he ordered the policeman. "Then call González, go to the rear courtyard, and dig a good, deep hole in the rear, where it's drier." He said it as if he'd been thinking up each word as he said it.

"And remember one messy thing for the rest of your life," he concluded. "This boy never died."

Two hours later they still hadn't finished digging the grave. From the balcony, the mayor realized that there was nobody on the street except for one of his men who was mounting guard from corner to corner. He turned on the stairway light and went to relax in the darkest corner of the anteroom, hearing only the spaced cries of a distant curlew.

Father Ángel's voice drew him out of his meditation. He heard him first talking to the policeman on guard, then to someone who was with him, and lastly he recognized the other voice. He remained leaning over in the folding chair, until he heard the voices again, inside the barracks now, and the first footsteps on the stairs. Then he reached his left arm out in the dark and grabbed the carbine.

When he saw him appear at the head of the stairs, Father Ángel stopped. Two steps behind was Dr. Giraldo, in a short jacket, white and starched, and a satchel in his hand. He displayed his sharpened teeth.

"I'm disappointed, Lieutenant," he said in a good humor. "I've been waiting all afternoon for you to call me to do the autopsy."

Father Ángel had his transparent and peaceful eyes fixed on him, and then he turned them on the mayor. The mayor smiled too.

"There'll be no autopsy," he said, "since there's no dead body."

"We want to see Pepe Amador," the curate said.

Holding the carbine barrel down, the mayor continued talking to the doctor. "I do too," he said. "But there's nothing we can do." And he stopped smiling when he told him:

"He escaped."

Father Ángel came up another step. The mayor raised the carbine in his direction. "Stay right where you are, Father," he warned. In his turn, the doctor advanced a step.

"Listen to one thing, Lieutenant," he said, still smiling. "It's impossible to keep secrets in this town. Ever since four in the afternoon on everybody knows that they did the same thing to that boy that Don Sabas did with the donkeys he sold."

"He escaped."

Watching the doctor, he barely had time to put himself on guard as Father Ángel came up two steps all of a sudden with his arms uplifted.

The mayor released the safety catch with a crisp blow by

the edge of his hand and remained planted with his legs apart.

"Halt," he shouted.

The doctor grabbed the priest by the sleeve of his cassock. Father Ángel began to cough.

"Let's play clean, Lieutenant," the doctor said. His voice hardened for the first time in a long while. "That autopsy has got to be done. Now we're going to clear up the mystery of the fainting spells prisoners have in this jail."

"Doctor," the mayor said, "if you move from where you are, I'll shoot you down." He barely turned his glance toward the priest. "And that goes for you too, Father."

The three remained motionless.

"Besides," the mayor went on, addressing the priest, "you ought to be pleased, Father. That boy was the one who was putting up the lampoons."

"For God's love," Father Ángel began to say.

The convulsive cough wouldn't let him go on. The mayor waited for the attack to pass.

"Now just listen to this mess," he said to them. "I'm going to start counting. When I reach three, I'm going to fire at that door with my eyes closed. Just be aware of that, now and forevermore," he warned the doctor explicitly. "The little jokes are over. We're at war, Doctor."

The doctor dragged Father Ángel away by the sleeve. He began his descent without turning his back on the mayor, and suddenly he began to laugh out loud.

"I like it this way, General," he said. "Now we really are beginning to understand each other."

"One," the mayor counted.

They didn't hear the next number. When they separated by the corner of the barracks, Father Ángel was demolished and had to turn his face away because his eyes were wet. Dr. Giraldo gave him a pat on the shoulder without ceasing to smile. "Don't be so surprised, Father," he told him. "All of this is life." On turning the corner by his house, he looked at his watch in the light of the lamppost: It was a quarter to eight.

Father Ángel couldn't eat. After curfew sounded he sat down to write a letter, and he was leaning over the desk until after midnight while the thin drizzle erased the world around him. He wrote in an implacable way, forming even letters with a tendency toward preciosity, and he did it with such passion that he didn't dip his pen again until he'd scratched out as many as two invisible words, scraping the paper with the dry pen.

On the following day, after mass, he put the letter in the mail in spite of the fact that it wouldn't go out until Friday. During the morning the air was damp and cloudy, but toward noontime it became diaphanous. A lost bird appeared in the courtyard and spent almost a half hour giving little invalid leaps among the spikenards. It sang a progressive note, rising up an octave each time until it became so sharp that one could only imagine it.

On his twilight walk, Father Ángel felt certain that all afternoon he'd been followed by an autumnal fragrance. At Trinidad's house, while he kept up a sad conversation about the infirmities of October, he thought he identified the smell that Rebeca Asís had exhaled in his study one night.

On his way back he'd visited Mr. Carmichael's family. The wife and eldest daughter were disconsolate, and whenever they mentioned the prisoner's name they hit a false note. But the children were happy without their papa's severity, trying to make the pair of rabbits that the widow Montiel had sent them drink from a glass. Suddenly Father Ángel had interrupted the conversation and, making a sign in the air, had said:

"Now I know: it's wolfsbane."

But it wasn't wolfsbane.

Nobody talked about the lampoons. In the hubbub of the latest happenings they were nothing but a picturesque anecdote of the past. Father Ángel had proof of it during his evening walk and after prayers, chatting in his study with a group of Catholic Dames.

When he was alone he felt hungry. He prepared himself some fried green banana slices and coffee with milk and accompanied it with a piece of cheese. The satisfaction of his stomach made him forget the smell. While he was getting undressed to go to bed, and then inside the netting, hunting the mosquitoes that had survived the insecticide, he belched several times. He had acid, but his spirit was at peace.

He slept like a saint. He heard, in the silence of the curfew, the emotional whispers, the preliminary testing of the chords tempered by the icy dawn, and lastly a song from another time. At ten minutes to five he realized that he was alive. He sat up with a solemn effort, rubbing his eyelids with his fingers, and thought: Friday, October 21. Then he remembered aloud: "Saint Hilary."

He got dressed without washing or praying. Having corrected the long buttoning of his cassock, he put on the cracked boots for everyday wear, whose soles were becoming detached. On opening the door to the spikenards, he remembered the words of a song.

" 'I'll be in your dreams till death,' " he sighed.

Mina pushed open the door of the church while he was giving the first ring. She went to the baptistery and found the cheese intact and the traps still set. Father Ángel finished opening the door onto the square.

"Bad luck," Mina said, shaking the empty cardboard box. "Not a single one fell today."

But Father Ángel didn't pay any attention. A brilliant day was breaking, with pure, clean air, like an announcement that in that year, too, in spite of everything, December would be punctual. Pastor's silence had never seemed more definitive to him.

"There was a serenade last night," he said.

"Of lead," Mina confirmed. "There was shooting until just a little while ago."

The priest looked at her for the first time. She, too, extremely pale, like her blind grandmother, wore the blue sash of a lay congregant. But unlike Trinidad, who had a masculine air, a woman was beginning to mature in her.

"Where?"

"All over," Mina said. "It seems they were going crazy looking for clandestine fliers. They say they lifted up the flooring of the barbershop, just by chance, and they found guns. The jail is full, but they say men are going into the jungle to join up with guerrilla bands."

Father Ángel sighed.

"I didn't notice anything," he said.

He walked toward the back of the church. She followed him in silence to the main altar.

"And that isn't anything," Mina said. "Last night, in spite of the curfew and in spite of the shooting . . ."

Father Ángel stopped. He turned his parsimonious eyes of innocent blue toward her. Mina also stopped, with the empty box under her arm, and she started a nervous smile before finishing the sentence.